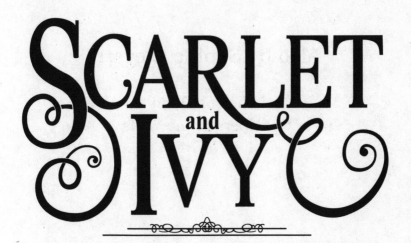

SCARLET and IVY

THE DANCE IN THE DARK

Also by Sophie Cleverly

The Lost Twin
Whispers in the Walls

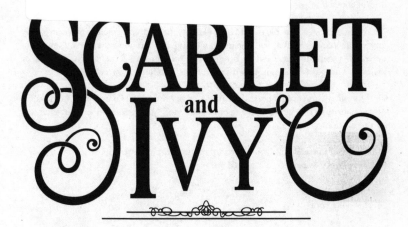

SCARLET and IVY

THE DANCE IN THE DARK

SOPHIE CLEVERLY

sourcebooks
jabberwocky

Published by Sourcebooks Jabberwocky, an imprint of Sourcebooks, Inc.
P.O. Box 4410, Naperville, Illinois 60567-4410
(630) 961-3900
Fax: (630) 961-2168
sourcebooks.com

Originally published in 2016 in Great Britain by HarperCollins Children's Books, an imprint of HarperCollins Publishers Ltd.

Library of Congress Cataloging-in-Publication Data

Names: Cleverly, Sophie, 1989- author.
Title: The dance in the dark / Sophie Cleverly.
Description: Naperville, IL : Sourcebooks Jabberwocky, [2018] | Series:
  Scarlet and Ivy ; [3] | Originally published in 2016 in Great Britain by
  HarperCollins Children's Books. | Summary: With a kindly new headmaster at
  Rookwood School, Scarlet and Ivy hope to focus on learning more about
  their mother but weird things start happening after a new ballet teacher
  arrives.
Identifiers: LCCN 2016030774 | (13 : alk. paper)
Subjects: | CYAC: Twins--Fiction. | Sisters--Fiction. | Secrets--Fiction. |
  Boarding schools--Fiction. | Schools--Fiction. | Mystery and detective
  stories.
Classification: LCC PZ7.1.C595 Dan 2018 | DDC [Fic]--dc23 LC record available at
  https://lccn.loc.gov/2016030774

Source of Production: Berryville Graphics, Berryville, Virginia, USA
Date of Production: March 2018
Run Number: 5011854

Printed and bound in the United States of America.
BVG 10 9 8 7 6 5 4 3 2 1

For all my Superheroes. The show must go on...

Chapter One

IVY

As new beginnings go, it was a good one.

The sun was making its first attempt at shining after the long, dark winter. I had my twin by my side—Scarlet was lounging on the grass, pretending it was warmer than it really was. Tall trees towered over us, their fresh buds stretching toward the sky.

And, well, we were back at Rookwood School. That part wasn't so good, but things were better than they were last term. Mrs. Knight, the interim headmistress, welcomed us in the foyer with a big smile on her face. The school hadn't had much luck with headmistresses and headmasters of late. Miss Fox was still on the run after being accused of embezzling money, not to mention hiding my sister in an asylum and pretending she was dead.

And Mr. Bartholomew had been no better. The cruel headmaster had finally been locked up for his involvement in the death of a student decades ago. Now the school was headless, so to speak, and Mrs. Knight was left in charge.

We'd had our first day of class of the spring term, and there hadn't been a caning in sight. All the teachers seemed happier. Even *Violet* seemed happier, and that was a feat in itself.

"Everything's rather good, isn't it?" I said to my twin with a happy sigh. I was a little chilly in my thin uniform, and the grass was damp, but the view down the long driveway of the school was beautiful now that everything was turning green again.

Scarlet looked up at me, unimpressed. "Aren't you forgetting something?"

I wasn't, but I was trying my hardest to be airy and cheerful. Of course, Scarlet had to bring me right back down to earth with a bang. *Ariadne.* Our best friend had been expelled before Christmas, after she was blamed for the fire Mr. Bartholomew had set to cover his tracks. Even after her name was cleared, her parents didn't want her coming back to Rookwood.

It felt like there was an Ariadne-shaped hole beside us. Several times that day I'd gone to tell her something or expected her to pipe up with a jolly comment only to be met with silence.

"I'm sure she's happy at home," I said weakly.

Scarlet sat up, grass stuck all down the back of her dress. "Oh, come on," she said, giving me a gentle shove. "Cheer up, Ivy. Things *are* better. Let's make a list." She pulled out her pen and a tattered notebook, the one she'd been using in place of her old diary. "One: no headteachers are going to try to murder us. Two: no more nasty punishments. Three: everyone's getting along. Penny has even stopped hating Violet."

Penny Winchester and Violet Adams were former archenemies of Scarlet, and they'd had their own massive falling-out last term. It was true they had finally made up, although that mostly involved not speaking to each other. "I'm not sure whether that should be on the list of good things," I said. "Do we really want them teaming up again?"

My twin chewed the end of her pen thoughtfully. "Good point. All right, scratch that one. Now we need a new number three."

"Well," I said, "Christmas was nice."

We'd been allowed to spend Christmas with our aunt Phoebe, Father's scatterbrained sister, after she'd found the courage to stand up to our meddling stepmother. I'd lived with our aunt for years before I came to Rookwood, when Scarlet was away at the school. Although I didn't like to admit it, she'd always seemed to prefer the company of my twin, which was rather strange given how opposite the two of them were.

"Three: Christmas," Scarlet said aloud as she jotted it down. As an afterthought, she added, "Excellent plum pudding."

I smiled. It had been so strange for me, seeing Scarlet in the cottage where I'd lived when I believed her to be gone forever. Strange but wonderful. I hadn't even minded when Aunt Phoebe burned the turkey or when she'd given me the exact same knitted scarf that she got me last year. This time, Scarlet got one too.

"Four," she said. "The weather is getting better."

"Ha!" I exclaimed. "Not as much as I would like. My dress is getting damp. And look at those clouds!"

Scarlet pouted at me and put the notebook away in her pocket. "Ah, but this is different. This is a new year. The promise of spring is in the air!"

She stood up, spread her arms wide, and took a deep, relaxing breath.

A raindrop landed on her nose.

We both laughed as we ran through the sudden downpour, back into the school and into our new beginning.

❧

Life went on. And for the first time, school was simple. The weather was a little warmer and brighter. Scarlet and I were awoken by the bell each day, went to class, ate a disappointing lunch, went to more classes, and

ate tasteless stew for dinner. Straight to bed with no
nighttime excursions.

I was happier, and I kept telling myself that. After
all, there were no secret diary trails, no ghosts to
hunt, no teachers waiting around the corner to give
us a caning. That was better, wasn't it?

One March morning, Scarlet sat down next to
me in assembly and practically slammed her head
on my shoulder. "Ivy," she declared. "I am utterly
bored."

I let out a sigh, glad I hadn't been the one to have
to say it. "Me too."

"For goodness' sake, let something interesting be
announced this assembly," she moaned.

"Like what?"

Nadia Sayani leaned over from the row behind.
"Perhaps an untimely death," she said, wiggling
her eyebrows.

"No!" I said. "No more untimely deaths!"

Nadia giggled and sat back again, and my twin
grinned mischievously. Then the teachers began
their usual round of shushing, so we sat up and paid
attention.

"Good morning, girls," said Mrs. Knight, then
waited for everyone to chorus their good mornings
back. Our head of house had often led assemblies
before, but it was somehow different now that she was
in charge of the school. "I have a special announcement for you today."

Our ears collectively pricked up.

"As I expect you all know, your practice examina-tions will take place at the end of this term..."

We all groaned. Surely this couldn't be the special announcement?

She waffled on for some time about the exams. Sunshine was spilling in through the hall windows. Even though it wasn't very warm outside, it was heating the room and all of us inside it, making me drowsy. I was usually a careful listener, but that day I tuned out most of her words.

"And now for the announcement," Mrs. Knight said in a more cheerful voice. "Miss Finch?"

I turned my gaze to the side of the stage and saw our ballet teacher. She had started using a cane recently, as her old injury was flaring up worse than ever. But nonetheless, she gave the hall a friendly smile as she climbed up to the lectern.

"Hello, girls," she said. "I'm pleased to announce that we will be having a special performance this term from the ballet students."

I grinned at my twin. That was us!

"They will be dancing the famous ballet *Sleeping Beauty*. The auditions will be held in a few weeks, and the roles will be chosen by a small judging panel of teachers."

I swear Scarlet clapped her hands in excitement, a gesture which reminded me a little of someone else.

"And if that wasn't exciting enough," Miss Finch

said playfully, "it will be taking place in the Theatre Royal in Fairbank. All students and parents will be able to purchase tickets, should they wish to."

Scarlet's eyes sparkled with the lights of fame. She was hooked, I could tell. This was her big chance at ballet stardom.

I was excited too of course—and nervous—but my excitement was dampened. My twin's enthusiastic response reminded me of the sad, Ariadne-shaped hole on the bench beside me. What was excitement if you had no best friend to share it with?

All Scarlet talked about was the ballet recital for the rest of the day. Especially in ballet class, where she spent more time going on about how brilliant it would be than actually practicing.

But my sadness was increasing. By the time we went up to our dorm room to get ready for dinner, I felt like crying.

"What *is it*, Ivy?" said Scarlet, plonking herself down on the bed beside me. "You've been quite the sourpuss all day. Aren't you *happy* about the ballet? It's what we've always dreamed of!"

It's what you've *always dreamed of,* I might have thought, but my mind was elsewhere. I was staring at my bedside table, where a pile of letters from my friend sat. I wasn't sure whether to admit to my twin what I really felt, but before I could stop myself, it came pouring out. "I miss Ariadne," I said. "I just wish she was here! Things are so dull without her!"

"Oh, *thank you very much*," said Scarlet. "Aren't I good enough for you?"

"You know what I mean," I replied.

She sighed and lay back on the bed, her head almost hitting the wall. "All right. I miss her too."

"There's got to be a way to get her back." I bit my lip. "I swore that I would. But after what Mrs. Knight said..."

"I know. Her father wants her to stay at home."

I undid my school tie and twisted it around my fingers. "It's not *fair*, is it? She did nothing wrong. Her father should let her come back if she wants to."

"He won't," said Scarlet. There was always a hint of anger in her voice when she spoke about it. "She's his precious daughter. He wants to wrap her in cotton wool and never let her out again."

It was hopeless.

✄

I blinked back tears as I walked down the hallway to the bathroom. I didn't want to be soppy in front of Scarlet. I'd only just convinced her that I wasn't as wet as she'd always thought I was.

But as I walked into the lavatories, I saw someone else I *really* didn't want to cry in front of.

Penny stared right at me. "Well, if it isn't the crybaby," she sneered.

I said nothing and tried to ignore her. She hadn't picked on me so far this term. I had been hoping it would stay that way.

"I'm talking to you, crybaby," she said. She shoved me, and I fell back against the cold sinks.

"Ow! What was that for?" I said.

"I'm sure you think you've won," she said, narrowing her eyes. "You and your sister may have got away with everything, but I don't forget."

Penny had a memory like a particularly vindictive elephant. Well, two could play at that game.

"I don't forget either," I said, trying to be brave. "I haven't forgotten that you tried to tell on us to the headmaster, or that you pushed Violet into the lake."

"We made up," snapped Penny. "It doesn't matter anymore."

"Then why are you picking on me again?" I asked. Every time I thought Penny had changed, her old horrible self reappeared just as quickly as it had gone.

"You're going to shut up and stay away from me," she growled. "Before I give you something to really cry about."

Chapter Two

SCARLET

Ivy seemed shaken when she came back into the room.

"What's up?" I asked.

"Nothing," she said. "Let's go down for dinner."

I shrugged. I guessed she was probably still getting herself upset about Ariadne. But what could we do? We didn't even know where Ariadne lived, so sneaking her away was out of the question. And I didn't think her father would be easily persuaded to change his mind.

We trudged downstairs, Ivy still being quiet. Maybe we were just going to have to move on. Ivy and I would be a team of two once more.

I took her hand and squeezed it gently, but she didn't squeeze back.

We made it to the dining room and joined the line. I

thought maybe a bit of humor might cheer up Ivy, so I put on my poshest voice. "What is it today, Miss?" I said to the dinner lady on duty, who was skinny as a rake and wearing a filthy apron. "Are we having *coq au vin*? Maybe some steak *tartare*?"

She frowned at me. "It's stew," she said.

I feigned surprise. "Really? How original! What will you come up with next?"

She dumped a ladleful on my plate, spilling half of it over the rim, and then thrust it toward me. "You'll eat what you're given," she said.

I nudged Ivy in the ribs. "I'm sure we'll enjoy this culinary delight, won't we, dear sister?"

"Hmm?"

Not even a giggle. The dinner lady was looking at me like she was about to put *me* in the stew. I sighed. "All right. *Fine.* I'll move along."

We got to our house table, Richmond, and I plonked my tray down.

Prefect Penny was already there, waving her fork around like she was conducting an invisible orchestra. "It will be simply magical," she was telling Nadia. "I have to be given the role of Aurora. It was practically made for me."

I glared at her. "Really? Because I'm pretty sure *I'm* the best ballerina here."

She turned to me, narrowing her freckle-rimmed eyes. "And, as I expected, Scarlet Gray is already jealous. She knows I'm perfect for the part."

I would have jumped across the table and slapped her if it wasn't for Ivy jamming her fork into my leg. "*Penelope*," I said bitterly. "The day you win the lead role in a ballet over me is the day Queen Victoria herself comes back from the grave and dances the Sugar Plum Fairy."

That got a few titters from around the table.

"Girls," said Mrs. Knight, bringing out her warning tone. "Let's be sensible, please."

Penny turned back to Nadia. "She's just bluffing," I heard her say quietly. "She knows she's not up to scratch."

I had to ignore them if I didn't want a talking-to from Mrs. Knight and another fork-stabbing from Ivy. So instead I just wolfed my stew down angrily. What did Penny know, anyway?

I lay awake that night worrying about Penny's stupid words.

Now, I know I shouldn't have given a care about the nonsense Penny came out with. But something she'd said had struck a chord.

She knows she's not up to scratch.

It was true. I was out of practice.

After all, I'd been locked in an asylum for months.

I shuddered and pulled the sheets up over my shoulders. I didn't want to think about the asylum again, not now, not ever. It was endless, horrible, and *dull* being trapped there. And worse, the feeling of abandonment, that I was never going to escape...

I shook my head into the pillow. Those thoughts had to be shut out.

I looked over at Ivy, wondering if I should wake her and ask her about my chances. She was snoozing peacefully, a half-finished book dangling from her fingertips. Somehow, I wasn't sure if I could. I always felt that I had to be the strong one, no matter how confident she got. And besides, she probably wouldn't understand. She loved ballet, but not for the same reasons I did.

For me, it was my dream. It was my ticket to fame and fortune. And I wasn't about to let anyone take it from me.

I *had* to be the best.

I *was* going to find a way to beat Penny and win that role.

Eventually, I don't know how or when, I fell asleep. And that was when the nightmare came.

I was onstage, the spotlight pouring onto me. There was no music, but I knew the dance anyway. I leaped and twirled, my limbs flowing gracefully.

But something was wrong. Someone out there in the darkness was watching me. Out of the corner of my eye, I kept catching a shadow dashing between the seats. In between each silent phrase of the score, it appeared and then vanished again.

I ground to a halt. I suddenly became aware that the theatre was full of people, all staring at me with blank faces. None of them could see the shadow as it passed behind them.

I shielded my eyes from the spotlight. "Who's there?" I called.

The shadow didn't reply. It was lurking, hiding. A person made of smoke, not flesh.

I looked around. I had stopped mid-performance. And now I couldn't remember where to start again.

From all around me came the sound of hissing.

It was the audience, I realized. They were hissing at me like snakes.

"No," I tried to say. "It's not my fault. I'm a good dancer! But there's something watching me! Can't you see it?"

The hissing got louder and louder, until it was deafening.

"No!" I yelled, and clamped my hands over my ears.

The shadow swooped out from behind a seat and began to stalk toward me.

And that was when I toppled from the stage and into the blackness below.

Chapter Three

IVY

If there was one thing Scarlet hated, it was not being the center of attention.

I'd had my taste of the spotlight when I was forced by Miss Fox to pretend to be my twin for a term at Rookwood School, and I'd found it *exhausting*. It brought stares and gossip and trouble. Especially from people like Penny.

But it hadn't been all bad. For the first time in my life I'd changed things and made things happen, and I had even made a real friend of my own. I'd felt noticed, like I was no longer just a reflection of my twin.

So, the center of attention was a nice place to visit, but I wasn't certain I wanted to *live* there.

The moment they announced the ballet recital, I knew Scarlet was going to obsess over the lead role. It was her chance to prove to everyone what she was worth, not just to our fellow students but to the teachers and parents and—just maybe, as she excitedly told me on the way to class that morning—potential ballet talent scouts. I honestly had no idea if there even was such a thing, let alone whether or not they came to school performances.

"I'm telling you," said Scarlet, "I'm the best ballerina in the school. Penny's nonsense doesn't faze me. She's like a parrot."

I wrinkled my nose. "Colorful and feathery?"

"No, you idiot!" Scarlet shot back, giving me a jab in the arm. "She's all squawk. She doesn't know what she's talking about. *Not up to scratch.* Pah!"

Scarlet was definitely protesting too much. She'd been yelling in her sleep, and I'd had a feeling she was dreaming about the auditions. Now I was worried too. The last thing I needed was for her rivalry with Penny to flare up again.

"I'm sure you could fit in some extra practice somewhere," I said.

Scarlet came to an abrupt stop outside the English classroom. "Practice?"

"That is traditionally how people do well at things," I pointed out.

"I don't need practice!" Scarlet snapped. "I'll wipe the floor with Penny. You'll see."

Our English teacher, Miss Charlett, peered out of the classroom door. "No wiping the floor with anyone, please," she said. "Come in, girls. You'll be pleased to hear we're beginning *Oliver Twist* today!"

I smiled, but Scarlet just rolled her eyes.

Behave, I mouthed at her, for all the good it would do. My sister's mind was firmly set on defeating Penny, and toeing the line was the last thing she cared about.

As if to prove me right, Scarlet got *three* detentions that day. She tried begging me to take them for her, but quickly gave up when she realized I was still cross about her attempt to persuade me to do it last term. Thankfully it now only meant writing lines, instead of a caning or worse.

As I passed Miss Fox's office on the way back to our room that afternoon, I saw Mrs. Knight standing in the doorway, talking to the caretaker—a middle-aged man with overalls and a bushy mustache.

"We really need to get rid of these," I heard her say, waving at the bizarre collection of stuffed dogs that still populated the office. "They're rather vulgar, aren't they?"

He scratched his head. "I s'pose we could sell them," he said. "To an antiques dealer, pr'aps."

I stopped, a sudden realization dawning. "You mean you haven't moved any of them, Miss?"

"Oh hello, Ivy," Mrs. Knight said, a little distracted. "No, the whole office has been left just as it was."

"Right," I said, frowning. "But, um, there was a Chihuahua on the desk, wasn't there?" I pointed to the little empty space where it had sat, which was now nothing but a slightly darker patch on the wood. "I remember it. It had pens in its mouth."

The caretaker grimaced, his lip twisting under his mustache. "Sounds unnatural to me."

Mrs. Knight looked puzzled. "You haven't touched anything, have you, Harold?"

He shook his head. "Can't say I like to go in there at all, Miss. Had to fix the window once and that old Miss Fox threatened to give me a whack with her cane if I wasn't quick enough. And all those dead mutts are enough to give any man the heebie-jeebies. Preferred to stay well clear, meself."

"It probably just got mislaid," said Mrs. Knight. "Perhaps when they were carrying out the investigation."

I nodded, remembering when I'd seen all the policemen going through her things. "That's probably it," I said. "Thank you, Miss."

"You're welcome," the acting headmistress replied. Then she blinked. I think she'd just realized that it was a bit strange of her to talk to a student about such things. "Go and get ready for dinner, then. Where's your sister?"

"Detention," I answered, feeling a spike of loneliness.

"Ah," she said.

I hurried away, leaving them both to discuss what to do with the unfortunate dogs.

But I couldn't help thinking that Mrs. Knight's explanation was odd. If that little dog wasn't in the office, given that everything else was still in its original place, then someone had deliberately taken it. And what would the inspectors want with a stuffed

Chihuahua that held pens? Come to think of it—who on earth would want it at all?

❧

I waited patiently in our room for Scarlet. I tried to do some prep work, but my mind wouldn't stay on task.

I thought about telling my sister, I really did. Twins are supposed to tell each other everything, and that was always what we had done...

Or at least, I'd thought so. Until I found out that Scarlet had swapped our exam papers to get into Rookwood School in the first place, because she'd known her marks wouldn't be good enough. Remembering things like that made me wonder if we could ever really trust one another again.

I doodled on my paper—only realizing halfway through that I'd drawn what looked like a tiny dog. I scratched it out.

I wouldn't tell Scarlet yet. There was no sense in worrying her. And I would keep quiet about Penny's threat too. Hopefully she would give up and leave me alone. It seemed unlikely though. As I passed her in the corridor just now she'd tried to trip me, her friends Ethel and Josephine breaking out in peals of laughter.

Around half-past five, my twin barreled back into our room.

"Finally!" I said, laying down my ink pen.

"*Pfft*," she replied, blowing a lock of hair out of her eye. "I'm so sick of detentions. I hate them."

"You realize there's a really simple solution to that, don't you?"

"And what's that then, Little Miss Know-It-All?" My twin dumped her satchel on to her bed, her workbooks spilling out of it.

"Stop getting into trouble!" Honestly, I wondered how we were related, sometimes.

"Oh, that. Well, *obviously*. I will. I've got the ballet recital to think about now," she said.

She had that to think about this morning, I thought, *and it didn't make a difference.*

"So," Scarlet continued, leaning over me to grab her silver hairbrush from the desk—the heirloom she'd inherited from our mother. "Anything interesting happen while I was gone?"

I felt my cheeks get a little warmer. "Nothing," I said. "It's been very uneventful."

My twin stared into the mirror as she brushed out her hair, which was the same dark brown as mine. "It's so strange," she said suddenly, "imagining our mother brushing her hair here."

"In this room?" I was skeptical. "Probably not."

"*No*, not in this exact room. But here, at Rookwood. Isn't that weird?"

I met my twin's gaze in the mirror and nodded. Last term we'd found out that our dearly departed mother couldn't have been who we'd thought she was. She had died shortly after we were born, and all we really knew about her was her name and her date of death: Emmeline Adel; February 26, 1914. But then we'd found those facts written on a memorial plaque for a girl who had drowned in the lake at Rookwood *over twenty years ago.* Whoever our mother was, it seemed she had been a Rookwood student, but she couldn't have been Emmeline Adel, who had met her unfortunate demise at the hands of the now-incarcerated headmaster, Mr. Bartholomew.

Scarlet looked down at the hairbrush in her hands. It had the initials **EG** on the back, for Emmeline Gray, our mother's married name. "I see this every day," she said, "and I just wonder...about everything. What was her real name? Who was she? If she cared. If she's... *watching* us now."

I shivered a little despite myself. "I don't know. I don't know if we'll ever know."

My twin put the brush down and posed in the mirror. "Do you think she'd be proud?" she asked.

That lightened my mood. "Ha! Proud of your three detentions in one day? Well, I suppose it's quite the achievement..."

Scarlet whacked me on the shoulder.

"Hurry up, smarty-pants. A horrible dinner awaits us once more."

I smiled. I could say one more thing about Mother—if Scarlet took after her, she must have been quite a character.

Chapter Four

SCARLET

I was practically buzzing when the time came for ballet class on Friday afternoon. My whole week had been building up to it.

"Come on, come on," I said to Ivy, dragging her through the corridor toward the studio.

"You don't have to drag me!" she protested. "I can walk myself!"

"Then walk faster! I have ballet to attend to!"

We reached the door that led down to the studio in the basement, only to find Miss Finch standing outside it. We were a little early, but it was unusual for her to not be inside already.

"Miss?" I said.

"Oh, good afternoon, girls," she said. "Go on down, I'll be right there." But her voice was shaky.

"What's the matter?" I asked. She was looking at

the stairway as if it were about to bite her, her walking stick clutched under one arm.

"Nothing, really," she said. "Don't worry. I just find the stairs a bit…difficult at the moment. I'll be all right."

Her brave face wasn't fooling me. "I'll go ahead," I told her, "and Ivy will be right behind you. Just in case…"

She smiled gratefully. "Thank you, girls."

I took the gaslit steps down into the basement, careful not to go too fast. It was still cold down there, as it had always been.

I reached the bottom and turned to watch our teacher take the last step. She grinned, though her face was pale and I could hear her breathing heavily. "Made it," she said triumphantly. "Go on. Since you're early, you can start your warm-up. I'll be grateful for my piano stool today."

Ivy and I went over to the *barre* and started our stretches. The rest of the class wasn't far behind.

Penny and Nadia walked in together, arm in arm. Penny looked annoyingly smug, and I fought the urge to make a cutting remark.

I was working through my *pliés* in each position, when I saw that Penny was smirking.

I looked down at my feet. Was I doing something wrong? No. I shook myself. It was a simple warm-up exercise, and one I had done a thousand times before, at that. I had to get Penny out of my head.

When we moved to center work, I didn't have to

look at her, as we all faced forward. That was fine, until we got to the *allegro* portion of the class, where we did the faster steps.

Miss Finch was instructing us from the piano, since she didn't feel up to demonstrating. I'd heard some of the other girls whispering, saying that she shouldn't teach a ballet class if she couldn't always dance. I thought she did a fine job, and I'd always tell them to shut up.

"We really need to work on our *pirouettes*, girls," she called. "They need to be polished for *Sleeping Beauty*, especially for whoever wins the role of Aurora."

We lined up in rows of three to practice, and, as luck would have it, I ended up with Ivy...and Penny. Ivy looked horrified, but I wasn't going to let it bother me. *Easy*, I thought. *I can do pirouettes in my sleep.*

I kept my eyes fixed and held my body tight. I lifted my back foot, held my arms out, and turned quickly, whipping my head around...

And I *spun*.

But I was off. Just a little. The realization that I was going to stumble hit me the minutest moment before it happened. I fell forward, my foot landing heavily on the wooden floor with a *thunk*.

My nightmare came flashing back. *Tumbling from the stage into the darkness.*

Penny laughed.

I stood up straight, fists clenched. I didn't know

who I was more furious with, myself or the freckled witch cackling next to me.

"Penny," Miss Finch chastised, "we don't laugh at others. Concentrate on yourself, please."

"Oh, but, Miss," Penny giggled. "Scarlet's definitely the best ballerina here. She told me so herself!"

And just to rub it in, Penny demonstrated a perfect *pirouette* right there and then.

Miss Finch still looked cross. "Ballet is about elegance and respect as much as it is about dancing. You're showing neither."

Penny bit her lip.

"Sorry, Miss," said Penny. "I'll stop it, I promise."

Ha. I gave her my stealthiest death glare. I knew she was thinking exactly the same as me: trouble in front of teachers would mean no lead role.

Things went from bad to worse. The mistake had completely thrown me off, and I just couldn't seem to get any of the steps. Ivy kept asking me if I was okay, and I wished she would shut up. I needed to be perfect, and I wasn't even close.

My turnout wasn't right. My toes weren't pointing as much as I wanted them to. My spins were wonky.

And all the while, Penny was smirking silently.

By the time we were curtseying to Miss Finch in *reverence,* I felt like screaming. What was wrong with me? I knew these moves by heart. Why wasn't my body cooperating?

I must really be out of practice, I thought, feeling

deeply, horribly embarrassed. The thought of getting it wrong onstage, of all those blank faces hissing at me...

That was when I had the idea.

"Ivy," I said, as we sat and unlaced our shoes. "Can you go on without me? I want to talk to Miss Finch."

Ivy looked a little baffled. "Why?"

"Oh well... I'm worried about her, and her leg, and all that." Which was the truth, just not the whole truth. "I thought I'd stay behind and see if she needs any help."

"I can help too," my twin said.

Drat.

"Well, I just... I'd just like to do something for her myself. You know, I still haven't made it up to her after the piano-smashing thing."

Ivy twisted her mouth, and I wasn't sure whether she was seeing through my excuses, or just thinking how stupid I'd been. During my first semester at Rookwood, I'd taken a mallet to Miss Finch's grand piano, then framed Penny for it. It hadn't been my finest hour.

"All right," said Ivy eventually, though she still looked unsure. "I'll see you later." I watched as she followed the rest of the girls out of the studio, and then wandered over to our teacher.

"Need any help, Miss?" I asked.

Miss Finch smiled at me. "I'll be all right, Scarlet, but thank you."

"Oh." I shuffled my feet.

"Did you want something, perhaps?" There was a twinkle in her eye. *Hmmph.* She'd seen right through me. I leaned back against her new piano and folded my arms.

"I..." I swallowed. The words didn't want to come out. "I think I need extra help." I felt my face heating up.

"You're just a little out of practice, that's all," she replied brightly. "You'll get it back again soon enough. It's just an off day. We all have those."

"But you could help me, couldn't you, Miss? Maybe just...some extra practice in the evenings?"

Her brow knitted. "I'm not sure about that. Wouldn't it be unfair to the other students? If this is about the recital... I'm one of the judges, you know. I can't be seen to be favoring anyone."

I racked my brain for a way to convince her. And then it hit me. "But...the reason I'm out of practice... is because of what happened, isn't it? Miss Fox—your mother—she had me *locked up*. That's got to be special circumstances. I've not had the same chance to learn as everyone else."

Miss Finch's face crumpled a little.

"Scarlet, I'm...I'm so sorry. I would have got you out sooner, if only I'd had any idea. You know that, don't you?"

I nodded, and chewed the corner of my lip.

She sighed. "Come back on Monday evening, after dinner. We'll see what I can do."

Chapter Five

IVY

I felt sure that Scarlet was up to something, but I couldn't say what. Perhaps she was just helping Miss Finch out of the goodness of her heart, but that didn't seem like a very Scarlet thing to do.

I didn't like being on my own. I walked down the corridor toward our room, and it felt strangely like my very first walk there—where I'd trailed along behind Miss Fox, believing my twin to be dead, not yet knowing Ariadne. The feeling left me hollow.

But worse was to come. Penny was leaning against our door, examining her fingernails.

"What are you doing?" I demanded. Suddenly, the fire I'd picked up from pretending to be Scarlet was back.

She looked up at me. "Alone again, are we? I'm beginning to think your twin doesn't like you."

"Penny." I glared at her. "Why are you leaning on our door?"

"Waiting for you," she said.

"You told me to stay away from you," I pointed out. "That's not easy if you're blocking the door to my room."

She ignored me. "Don't you wonder what she's up to without you? Getting herself in more trouble, do you think?"

"You wish," I said. "You just want to stop her getting that part in the ballet, don't you?"

"Oh, I don't *want* to," said Penny. "I *know* I will. And you're going to help me." Suddenly she stepped forward and pushed me back against the wall. "She'll do anything to protect you, won't she?"

"Let go of me!" I yelled, but it came out more weakly than I'd hoped, more of a squeak than a roar. I looked around the corridor desperately. A group of first years were passing, but they huddled away, looking terrified.

I could really use your help, Scarlet, I thought.

But then again... Penny was right. Scarlet would flip if she saw this. Could I risk that? She could lose that part. Worse, she could be kicked out of school, and then I'd really be alone...

"I mean it, Penny," I tried again, louder this time, but with my voice shaking.

A door farther down the corridor opened, and Nadia peered out. "Penny?" she called. "What are you doing?"

Penny dropped me like a hot iron. My uniform was crinkled from where she'd pinned me against the wall. "Just helping Ivy fix her tie," she called back, a sickly sweet grin on her face. She turned back to me and winked. *Ugh.*

As she stalked off to meet Nadia, I took a deep breath. Shortly afterward, Scarlet appeared at the top of the stairs. She sauntered over to me.

"What took you so long?" I asked. I couldn't mention what had just happened. She'd chuck Penny out of the nearest window. "I still don't understand why you needed to talk to Miss Finch so badly. Is something up?"

"Nope," she said all too casually. "Nothing at all."

⨯

"Is something up?" I asked Scarlet again, as we brushed our teeth in the chilly school bathroom. I still wasn't convinced things were okay.

"*Blurble*," she replied, her mouth full of toothpaste.

"What?"

"I *said*, no!" She slammed down her regulation toothbrush, which had PROPERTY OF ROOKWOOD SCHOOL stamped into the handle. "Nothing is up, just as it has not been the last five times you asked. Let's just go to bed, all right?"

"All right. Fine."

Scarlet was soon snoring, but I lay awake,

watching the moonlight dance on the walls through the thin curtains.

There was something troubling me, and it wasn't just Penny. I still hadn't mentioned the missing stuffed dog. I'd been trying not to think about it or about anything to do with Miss Fox. She was long gone, I had to remember that.

And that was when I heard it.

Out in the corridor, an unmistakable sound. One I thought I'd never hear again.

The clacking of heels, and the jangling of keys in pockets.

No. Oh no.

"Scarlet!" I whispered, panicked. "Scarlet!"

The sound echoed past, louder and then quieter, as if she were walking right by our door.

It can't be!

"*Scarlet!*" I leaped out of bed and dived into my twin's, grabbing her blanket and pulling it over my head, my heart racing.

"*Unf,*" she said, giving me a sleepy shove. "What is it? I'm trying to sleep."

"I heard...I heard..." I stopped, gasping for breath, and listened.

The sound was gone. I could hear nothing except my twin's breathing, and my own.

"...heard what?" Scarlet asked, putting her head under the blanket next to mine. "What's the matter?"

"I..." I frowned. Surely I was imagining things. "I

don't know. Sorry. I think I might have been having a nightmare."

"You *are* a nightmare," she replied. "But if it'll calm you down, you can stay over here."

"A-all right," I said. "'Night, Scarlet."

"'Night, Ivy," she murmured. She turned over to face the wall, taking most of the blanket with her.

I rolled on to my side, but my panic refused to fade. Could you dream a *sound*? Perhaps you could. It was late, after all, and dark, and I was tired.

I tiptoed over to the door, opened it, and cautiously peered out. There at one end of the corridor was the matron, holding a bunch of keys. She yawned, unlocked the door to her room, and stepped in.

I leaned back, breathless with relief. It was only the matron. There was nothing to worry about.

�֍

Scarlet seemed more cheerful the next morning, perhaps because it was the weekend.

I didn't want to spoil it by blabbing about my worries, and if I said a word about Penny, Scarlet would surely go mad, so I left things well alone.

"Let's go and find Rose," suggested my twin at breakfast. "I haven't seen her in forever!"

"Well, she doesn't go to class, does she?" I said. "She's not even officially a student."

Nadia leaned in. "I think she's down at the stables

most days. I heard Mrs. Knight saying she's a natural with horses. Happy to muck them out, apparently!" She pulled a face.

We'd met Rose last term, when Violet had rescued her from the asylum—we'd never quite figured out whether it was true friendship or the promise of a family fortune that had motivated Violet. Rose, a mysterious girl, had always loved horses and ponies, and we'd even found Rose in the stables one night when she'd escaped the hidden room where she'd been staying.

Ariadne loved ponies too, I thought. I felt another pang of loneliness for our missing friend. Perhaps a visit to Rose would help.

As soon as we'd gulped down our porridge, we headed outside to the stable yard. It was a warm day, with the sun peeking through the clouds and a hint of spring (and only a little drizzle) in the air. We tramped through the mud and straw that lay scattered on the ground.

I spotted Rose's blond hair over the top of one of the stable doors.

"Hello, Rose," I said.

She looked up, stepped out of the stall, and waved a shovel at me. Rose wasn't usually one for words.

"How are the horses?" I asked.

I wasn't sure if Rose would answer at first, but she had been getting a little better at talking lately— especially if it was to do with horses. She twisted her golden locket nervously before tucking it inside her sweater.

"Good," she replied decisively. Then she paused, and stared back at the stall she had just come out of. "This one isn't hungry," she added quietly.

Scarlet snorted. "I'm going to go and give one a new hairstyle," she said, grabbing a brush and wandering off across the yard.

But she hadn't noticed which horse Rose was talking about.

Stall number four. *Raven.* The big black horse that belonged to...

Miss Fox.

I stepped closer to Rose and lowered my voice. "Why isn't he hungry?" I asked.

Rose leaned the shovel back against the wall, then gestured at me to follow her over to the stable door. She pointed inside.

Raven was lazing in the far corner, lying down and looking—though perhaps it was just my imagination—a little fatter than he had before. But what I wasn't imagining was what Rose was trying to show me: there were bits of treats left scattered in the straw. A carrot top. An apple stalk. A few loose shavings where the big horse's teeth had carved slices off the veg.

It was clear from the puzzled expression on Rose's face that she wasn't responsible for them.

"Maybe it was the other girls," I said, trying to

reassure us both. "Maybe some of the first years thought they'd give him some extra treats."

Rose nodded, her long blond locks bobbing gently. "They do that sometimes," she whispered.

"Look!" Scarlet called from across the yard. She'd plaited a horse's hair over its eyes. I sighed and walked over to her. "Scarlet? Remember not getting into trouble?"

My twin just grinned. "The horses can't make me write lines," was all she said.

Chapter Six

SCARLET

The weekend had been fun, but for once I couldn't wait for it to end. We'd walked to the village shop and bought midnight feast sweets, as was our tradition, even if it felt strange to do it without Ariadne.

But I was waiting for Monday. Not only would I get to do ballet, but I'd also get my extra practice with Miss Finch.

I was restless for most of the day, but I made sure to not get in *too* much trouble. The last thing I wanted was another blasted detention.

At least Ivy had stopped incessantly asking me what was on my mind. I knew I ought to say something, but there was a lot I *ought* to do.

Ivy tells you everything, my brain insisted.

Pfft. It wasn't as if my extra practice would have to be a secret forever. Just until I got the part.

Ballet was the last class of the day, and I felt both excited and, well, a *little* nervous.

To my relief, everything went fairly smoothly—even queen witch Penny seemed to be on her best behavior. We practiced a small section from the beginning of *Sleeping Beauty.*

But I couldn't stop second-guessing myself. Was my leg as straight as Nadia's? Were Ivy's jumps higher than mine? I didn't even dare look at Penny, because if she was any better than me, I didn't want to know.

It's all fine, I told myself over and over. *You'll get your extra practice. Then you'll be the best.*

It was all I could do to not say anything to Miss Finch when the lesson was over. I really wanted to make sure she hadn't forgotten, or worse, changed her mind. But if I said anything, I'd give myself away. It'd be one thing if Ivy found out, but I couldn't risk Penny knowing. I'd be utterly humiliated.

So, Ivy and I traipsed back to room thirteen, and I pretended nothing was different.

"Oh!" I yelled suddenly, as we reached our door.

"What?" asked Ivy.

I spread my empty hands out wide. "I forgot my toe shoes. I must have left them in the studio."

My twin looked exasperated. "What's wrong with you this week? You never forget your shoes." Her own soft pink shoes were dangling from her arm.

"Dunno," I said. "Anyway, it doesn't matter. I'll go back down and get them. I'll see you in a bit."

"Try to make it back before dinner," she replied.

You'll be lucky, I thought.

∽

I was almost out of breath by the time I reached the studio. What if Miss Finch changed her mind? I *had* rather guilt-tripped her into it...

But there she was, sitting at her piano stool, just as she always did.

"I'm back!" I announced.

She smiled at me. "I can see that. Let's get started."

She watched as I pirouetted over and over, trying to get it just right.

"Engage your core muscles," she said. "Keep your eyes up."

Every time I did a pirouette, I felt a little less dizzy and a little more confident. But I was still wobbling.

"You don't need to push yourself quite so hard. You'll throw the turn off. You're not trying to spin as fast as you can." She pointed to my head. "Imagine yourself doing it perfectly, in a controlled way."

I took a deep breath, and made sure my starting *plié* was right. That final time, I spun the *pirouette* without a wobble.

"Excellent!" said Miss Finch, clapping her hands. "Keep it up. I think that's enough for now."

I had to say something. "Miss?"

"Yes?"

I couldn't quite meet her eye. "I'm sorry if I made you feel bad. What Miss Fox did to me wasn't your fault. I hope you don't think you have to help me just because of that."

She looked up, her eyes searching my face. "Oh, Scarlet. It's quite all right. You haven't had as much time as the other girls, so I don't mind doing this bit extra for you."

"Are you sure?" I really wanted that to be true.

"I'm sure. Now come on, you need to get up to dinner. There's still time if you go quickly."

"Yes, Miss! Thank you, Miss!" I beamed.

"Don't forget to get changed," she said with a grin. That was a good point. I'd get all manner of questioning if I turned up at the dinner hall in my ballet clothes. Not to mention I'd probably never get the smell of stew out of them. "I'll see you again on Friday."

"Thank you," I said again. I was repeating myself, but I meant it. This time she didn't reply, just went back to happily playing the piano.

Things were finally looking up.

When I reached our dorm, Ivy had already gone to dinner without me. I threw my uniform back on and headed down to the dining hall to join her.

She was not entirely pleased.

"Where on earth have you been?" she demanded loudly over the racket of the hall as I slid into my seat. "I was worried sick!"

"I just..." I started. "I went to get my shoes back from the studio, and I got talking to Miss Finch."

My twin looked skeptical. "Well, it was a long talk," she said. "You were gone forever. I was getting anxious."

"Oh, come on," I said, slamming down my knife and fork. "Can't I do anything on my own without you having a panic about it?"

Ivy gave me the look that she'd developed recently: the one that said *I thought you were dead, so cut me some slack.*

But this time it wasn't going to work. I was fed up of her using that as an excuse to keep tabs on me. "I was *fine*," I said pointedly. "We were just talking about the ballet recital. Nothing happened. This school isn't dangerous anymore!"

Mrs. Knight suddenly appeared behind Ivy. "You're quite right, Scarlet. Rookwood is a safe place for everyone, I will be making sure of that!"

I looked up at her. She'd said that as if she'd been practicing in front of a mirror.

"Uh...thank you, Miss?" said Ivy.

It was quite unusual for Mrs. Knight to join in our conversations. She seemed to register our surprise. "Yes," she said, "I think it's important that everyone knows how *different* things are these days."

"You mean now that headteachers aren't trying to murder us anymore?" I asked.

"Scarlet!" She looked affronted. "Well, really!"

Nadia looked up. "She's not lying though, Miss. At least one of them was a murderer. The other—"

"That's quite enough," snapped Mrs. Knight. "This is a *new* Rookwood School, and I won't hear any more about the past. Let's all move forward, please."

"Yes, Miss," we chorused. She bustled away, her cheeks red.

We ate our dinner quietly after that. At least Mrs. Knight's interruption had saved me from any further interrogation by Ivy. But how long could I keep my extra ballet lessons a secret? Maybe Mrs. Knight wasn't going to try to kill me, but if Ivy found out I'd been lying to her…it wasn't going to end well.

Chapter Seven

IVY

That evening, I lay in my lukewarm bath and tried as hard as I possibly could to stop worrying.

It wasn't working out particularly well. Just being in the bathrooms always reminded me of the first time I'd set foot in there, when I'd been hunting for one of the pieces of Scarlet's diary. When I'd first come to Rookwood School, I'd truly believed that she was dead, and that the paper trail she'd scattered was all that was left of my sister. It made my toes curl just thinking about it.

And worse—just after I'd found the pages, I'd been ambushed by Penny. Even if we were truly safe from the teachers, Penny was still desperate to give me nothing but trouble.

I shivered as I climbed out of the bath and wrapped myself in a threadbare towel. It was times like these that I really missed my Aunt Phoebe's house. There was something so comforting about the tin bath in front of the fire, even if you had to fill it yourself with the kettle.

As I changed into my nightgown, I had the idea to write to my aunt. I made sure to do so every now and again, even if her replies often didn't entirely make sense.

I peered around the corner before I left the bathroom, just in case Penny was lurking. Thankfully, she wasn't.

Scarlet was already back in our room, practicing ballet. There really wasn't much room, but that didn't stop her.

"Don't mind me," she said.

"I won't," I snapped back, dodging around her to get to my bed. I still hadn't forgiven her for disappearing earlier.

My twin just ignored me and carried on doing *pliés*. Typical.

I reached under my bed and pulled out my satchel, where I had some sheets of paper and a pencil. At least I could write letters without having to worry about them being intercepted by the teachers anymore.

Dear Aunt Phoebe,

I hope this finds you well. I miss you.
Thank you for having us to stay at
Christmas. If you can't find the turkey

knife, it's because Scarlet was using it to try and carve a sword out of a branch.

Things seem to be better here at school. Mrs. Knight says we're all safe and I hope that's true, but some things have happened that are making me worried... Perhaps I'm overthinking it. I don't want to scare Scarlet, or make her angry.

Speaking of Scarlet, she's been

"Are you writing about me?" said my twin suddenly, her face appearing over the top of my paper. I jumped so quickly that I almost crumpled the whole page into a ball.

"Scarlet! Go away! It's private!"

"Private?" she frowned. "Since when? You're only writing to Aunt Phoebe."

I flattened the paper against my nightgown so that she couldn't read it. "How do you know that?"

"Who else would you be writing to? You already wrote to Ariadne just the other day, so unless you've suddenly decided to try and rebuild our relationship with Father, I assume you're writing to Aunt Phoebe. Come on, let me see—"

"*Scarlet!*" This was exasperating beyond belief. "When you vanish for an hour I'm apparently prying if I want to know where you've been, but then you demand to read my letters! How is that fair?"

"Hmmph," she said, and threw herself down on her

bed, unlacing her ballet shoes so hastily I thought she was going to break them. "I just think that *sometimes* we should share things. Maybe not *all* the time." She chucked the shoes at the chair.

I glared at her. I knew exactly what she meant. She meant that we should share everything when it suited her, and not otherwise. "I'm going to sleep," I said finally.

"Fine. Me too."

"Brilliant."

There was a long pause, as both of us lay back on our beds and stared at the ceiling, flooded with anger that neither of us wanted to release.

"Ivy?"

"What?"

"The light's still on."

"Oh."

With a sigh, I climbed up and went over to flick off the light switch. Room thirteen was plunged into darkness. Even the moon wasn't shining that night but was buried under gray clouds.

Back in my bed, on my blessedly no-longer-quite-so-lumpy mattress, I tried desperately to sleep. Unfortunately though, sleep is one of those things where trying desperately to achieve it only results in it never happening.

I turned to look at my twin, but I could barely make out her shape, just a lump of blanket. So, I stared up at the ceiling instead, until eventually I drifted off into a peculiar dream. One that I'd had a few times in the past month or so, but each time it altered slightly, unnerving me even more.

I was standing on a hill, green grass waving softly around my feet. I could feel the summer heat on my back. The sky was blue, the sun blindingly bright.

There was someone in front of me, sitting in the grass on a threadbare picnic blanket.

It was a woman, and I felt sure, somehow, that it was our mother.

She never turned around. She just sat there, a black silhouette against the sky. I tried to move toward her, to touch her, but I was rooted to the spot. I called her name—Emmeline—but my voice faded to nothing in the breeze. She couldn't hear me.

Or perhaps—I realized, in the strange way you think in your sleep—it was the wrong name?

She wasn't Emmeline, was she? Emmeline had died when she was just a girl.

Mother! I called, trying to pull my feet from the ground, but it was as though they had grown into the grass, the roots pulling me down. Mother! I'm here!

Still the figure didn't turn.

I slept on…

⁂

And then, in the middle of the night, I awoke with a start.

Someone was trying our door handle.

I watched, sick with horror, as it turned. Time slowed to a crawl. Scarlet didn't even stir in the opposite bed.

The door creaked open, just a fraction.

"Who...who's there?" I whispered, as loudly as I dared.

The door thumped back into place, and the handle sprang up.

And I could have *sworn* I heard the jangling of keys in pockets and the clacking of heels as someone hurried away.

Chapter Eight

SCARLET

I thought I'd been the one acting strangely that week, but Ivy was really taking the cake.

When I woke up on Tuesday morning, she was sitting by our dorm room door and staring at it as if it were about to sprout legs and walk away.

"What are you doing, you oddball?" I murmured sleepily.

"Nothing," she said, but she looked guilty about it. She was quiet and jumpy for the rest of the day. I only had to speak to her and she would flinch as if I'd given her a slap. In biology, Mrs. Caulfield asked her to get something from the cupboard and she just started panicking.

"Miss, I can't, I'm...not feeling well!" she said and ran out of the classroom.

When classes were over, I cornered her in the

corridor. "What *happened* last night? Did someone kidnap my sister and replace her with a total wimp?"

She opened her mouth and gawped at me like a stunned fish. For a moment, I expected her to start yelling—ever since we'd been reunited, she'd been so much more...well, like me. She'd stand up for herself, argue back.

But now...it was like the old Ivy had reappeared. She looked like she wanted to shrink into the wall. I watched her face carefully.

"I—" she started, then bit her lip. "Actually," she said, "there was something. I keep having this *dream*."

I took her arm as we started to walk back to our dorm, steering her through the crowds of uniformed girls. "Tell me about it."

"It's about our mother, I...I think. I'm on this hill, and she's sitting there in front of me, but I can't see her face. And I can't get her to turn around."

I shrugged—as much as you can shrug with your arm through someone else's. "All right, it sounds weird, I admit. I've had some pretty unusual dreams myself recently. That doesn't seem particularly scary or anything." I was thinking of my nightmares with the dark stage, but I swiped the thought away before it could bother me.

We climbed the stairs slowly. "It just...it feels so wrong," she said. "Like *I'm* doing something wrong. Because no matter what I do, I can't get to her. And she won't listen to me."

"Well, she is dead," I said, but the look on my twin's face told me that was not a very tactful thing to say. "Sorry."

"I know. But I had a realization—I kept calling her Emmeline. At first I thought that maybe it's not her, maybe it's the shadow of someone else." I shuddered. "But if she wasn't *called* Emmeline, then..."

I snapped my fingers, almost right in the face of Ethel Hadlow, who glared at me as she passed. "You don't know her real name. So, that's why you can't get her attention!"

"I-I think that might well be it," Ivy said. "Not that the dream is real, or anything, but..."

"But it made you think, yes?" We reached room thirteen, and I went to turn the door handle. I could've sworn Ivy flinched at that too.

"Yes," she said, after a moment. "There's got to be a way to—"

"Hello!"

Both of us nearly jumped out of our skin.

It was Ariadne.

She was sitting on my bed. Ivy backed up against the wall, gasping.

"Ariadne?" we exclaimed.

"I'm sorry!" she said, hurriedly jumping to her feet. "I didn't mean to be scary. Was I scary?"

"Only mildly terrifying," I replied, my heart thumping a little. I hadn't expected anyone to be there, let alone our absent friend.

"Sorry!" she said again. "Well...hello." She looked sheepish.

I bounced over to her. "Come on," I said, "we'll need a bit more than that. You were *expelled*! What are you doing here?"

"I came back," she said, as if that weren't evident from her standing right there in the middle of our room.

"But how?" said Ivy, before we both hugged Ariadne.

"Mmf," Ariadne said, so we stopped squeezing her quite so much and stood back a little to give her some air. "Well," she said triumphantly, "I persuaded Daddy. Since they found out it was the headmaster who started the fire in the library and not me, the school had no objection to letting me in again."

"But Mrs. Knight said there was no way your father would let you come back. Because he thinks it's too dangerous for you to go outside or something."

"Well, I...*might* have threatened to tell Mummy that he ran over her prize petunias when he was trying out the new Bentley." Ariadne carried on staring at her feet, her face red.

Ivy's eyes widened. "You blackmailed your father?"

"Oh no! I mean, it's not blackmail, is it? Well, he shouldn't have done it in the first place. He's not even supposed to drive a motor car, that's Horace's job..." Her mouth kept on flapping uselessly.

"Ariadne, you silly thing!" I shook our friend gently by the shoulders. "It doesn't matter if you locked him in the basement to get back here. You did it!"

Her face lit up. "I did it! I'm back!"

I ran out into the corridor, nearly tripping over the little trail of suitcases. "Ariadne's back!" I yelled to no one in particular.

Penny leaned out of the doorway of her room and glared at me. "Nobody cares!" she shouted.

But even wicked witch Penny couldn't dampen my mood. We were a proper team again. This was *utterly brilliant.* I danced into room thirteen and spun Ariadne around.

"Bit dizzy now, Scarlet!" she said primly, and I let her go.

Ivy was grinning like a loon. "I can't believe it," she kept saying.

I sat down at the vanity and blew a lock of hair off my face. "So," I said, "where are they putting you, now that Violet and Rose are roomies?"

"Apparently, I'm to go in one of the bigger dorms with the seventh graders," Ariadne said. She went out into the corridor and picked up one of her suitcases. "I'm actually rather excited. They'll love my midnight feasts, don't you think?"

Ivy laughed. "I'm sure they will," she said.

"Oh, *wonderful,*" said Ariadne, sinking onto the bed in relief. "Anyway," she said suddenly, "did I interrupt you? You were talking about something..."

Ivy sat down on her bed. "I was thinking about our mother," she said. "I had this dream about her, and—Oh! You don't know!"

"Know what?" Ariadne asked.

Ivy gave me a quick glance—neither of us had explained. Nor had we put it in our letters. The truth had seemed too strange and secret to risk the teachers finding out, even the good ones. "After you were expelled, we went looking for the memorial plaque to the girl who drowned in the lake. And we found it, but it wasn't exactly what we were expecting..." I paused, not wanting to waste a good moment for dramatic effect. "The name on it was *our mother's*. Or at least, what we thought was our mother's."

"Your mother was a ghost?" exclaimed Ariadne. Her voice was reaching peak squeakiness levels.

"No, no." Ivy waved her hands desperately. "At least, I don't think so. We think that Emmeline Adel must not have been her real name."

"Hmm." Ariadne wrinkled her nose. She looked utterly baffled. "Well, who was she then?"

"Not the faintest," I said. "A student at this school, I suppose. That's as much as we know."

"Oh!" said Ariadne suddenly. "Was she one of the Whispers, do you think?"

That was a good point. Last term, when we'd discovered Rose hiding in the secret room below the library, we'd also uncovered the Whispers in the Walls. They were a top-secret club that, twenty years ago, had vowed to bring down Headmaster Bartholomew and reveal the truth about what he'd done to the students of Rookwood—including the murder of the real Emmeline Adel. We'd had their book full of coded writing, but it had been destroyed in the fire, along with the staircase down to the secret room.

"I suppose she might well have been," Ivy replied. "If only we hadn't lost that notebook..."

"I might be able to remember some of the names from the wall," Ariadne said, in between thoughtfully chewing on one of her nails.

Suddenly, an idea flashed brightly in my mind. "We ought to talk to Miss Jones! She went to school here, didn't she? She might have known our mother!"

Ivy beamed at me. "That's a brilliant idea!"

"Um, I think she's away," said Ariadne. "I went past the library earlier and I didn't see her in there."

"She probably needed some time off," said Ivy. "She was really upset about the library. It was in such a state after the fire."

I hadn't been there yet, but Ivy said it still smelled faintly of smoke, and a lot had had to be replaced. Miss Jones had been totally distraught about the loss of her precious books.

I went over and patted Ariadne on the back. "Dinner?" I said.

"Oh! Yes!"

I grinned. If Ariadne had missed Rookwood's school dinners, there was definitely something wrong with her!

∾

Miss Jones the librarian was indeed away that week, Mrs. Knight confirmed at the Richmond dining table. Our inquisition would have to wait.

The days leading up to Friday were a blur as I counted down the hours to my next secret ballet session. And of course, I had to come up with a way to distract Ivy. There was no way she was going to believe me if I tried to use the shoe excuse again.

Things got even more tricky when I happened to pass Miss Finch in the hallway. "Ah, Scarlet," she said. "Could you come down after dinner on Friday? I think I'll need a bit of a longer rest after the lesson."

"Yes, Miss," I said, a lot more brightly than I felt. "I'll see you then."

∾

On Friday, our ballet class flew by, almost quite literally, as were practicing *tour jetés*. I felt that I was getting better—but was I good enough?

I gave Miss Finch a little wave as class finished, not daring to be any more obvious. And I barely touched my dinner—which was part of the plan, but honestly, I felt too nervous to eat.

"What's wrong, Scarlet?" Ivy asked. "I know you hate the stew, but it's not actually that bad today."

"I don't feel well," I said. "I think I might...be sick." I gagged a little for effect.

"Goodness," said Mrs. Knight. She edged her chair backward as if I were about to spew all over her. "To the sick bay, quickly!"

I nodded, pushed my chair back and hurried out of the hall. I felt ashamed seeing the worried looks on Ivy and Ariadne's faces. There was some chuckling from Penny's direction, but I tried to ignore it. It was better than her knowing what was really going on.

I rushed through the corridors, pulling my ballet outfit out of my satchel as I went. I had to dart into an empty classroom and tug on my leotard and tutu. As I stuffed my uniform into the bag, I *really* hoped no one would try to check up on me in the sick bay. I decided to leave my bag hidden behind a desk and come back for it later.

I made it to the door of the ballet studio, which was swinging open, and peered down the stairs.

All was quiet. I couldn't hear the tinkle of Miss Finch's piano keys or any sound of her walking around. It suddenly seemed a little *too* quiet.

Come on, Scarlet, I told myself. *Don't be a wet blanket.*

I took a deep breath and the first step.

And as I got nearer, I realized what else was wrong. It was dark.

The gas lamps that always burned brightly in the studio were out.

I felt my heart speed up.

"Miss?" I called. "Miss Finch?"

There was no reply.

At the bottom of the stairs, there was a small candle holder on the wall. I fumbled for it, and found a waxy stub with the wick still intact, and a match balanced on the side. I tried to stay calm, but my hand shook as I struck the match on the wall and lit the candle. A flame sputtered to life.

I held it out in front of me, and I saw...

Myself and the candle, reflected a million times in the mirrors.

The piano, the stool tipped on its side.

And Miss Finch's walking stick, lying in the middle of the floor...

Chapter Nine

IVY

Scarlet flung open the door of room thirteen and strode in.

She found me sitting on the bed, arms folded. "Where have you been?" I demanded.

She looked at me crossly. "I was ill, remember? I went to the sick bay."

I stood up. "Except you didn't. Ariadne and I hurried up there as soon as we could to see if you were all right! Nurse Gladys said she hadn't even seen you!"

My twin just glared at me. She hated being caught out in a lie. "It doesn't matter," was all she said.

"It *does* matter," I shot back. I wanted to tell her that I was afraid something had happened to her again. The things I'd been seeing and hearing around school had only made it worse.

"Leave it," she warned, throwing herself on her bed.

Suddenly, I noticed something strange. "You weren't wearing your ballet outfit before!"

Her face was in her pillow, but she tipped it toward me. "I said it doesn't matter. I just wanted to do some ballet, alone, all right?"

"Fine," I said. "Well, I'm going to tell Ariadne that you're not sick, and then I'm going to have a bath and brush my teeth, *alone*."

"I don't need to know every detail of your life," she grumbled.

Hmmph. I got up, picked up my things and headed toward Ariadne's new dorm. It was some way down the corridor, in the section with the larger dorms for first years.

Unfortunately, I forgot that visiting Ariadne also meant going past Penny's door.

I shut my eyes and held my breath as I walked, as if this would somehow protect me. But as soon as I approached, Penny's door was yanked open. "So, is your sister terribly ill, or do I need to tell everyone that she's just pretending? I don't know which I'd prefer."

"Shut up, Penny," I said, and kept on walking.

"So, she's fine?" Penny put on a mock expression of horror. "And she *lied* to a teacher?" She pulled out her prefect book and waved it at me. "I'll be writing that one down."

I dug my shoes into the worn hall carpet. "Mr. Bartholomew's gone. You're not his stupid prefect anymore."

"I'm still a prefect, *Gray*," she snapped back. "Which means I can do no wrong." She smiled sweetly, the kind of sweetness from eating too many chocolates that leads to you being sick. "See you soon." She slammed the door.

I gritted my teeth. *Ignore her*, I told myself as I walked on. *Count to ten.*

Thankfully, once I got to ten, Ariadne came out of her dorm, carrying her Rookwood regulation towel, toothbrush, and soap. Relieved, I hurried over.

"Ariadne!" I called out. "Scarlet's fine. She's in a complete huff, but otherwise unharmed."

"Oh, phew," my friend said, tucking a lock of mousy hair behind her ear. "Where did she go?"

"No idea," I said. "Something to do with ballet. She won't say."

Ariadne shrugged, nearly dropping her towel in the process. "Are you going to the bathrooms too?"

I nodded. "Let's go together. I don't want to run into...anyone. Else."

Ariadne looked at me strangely, but she didn't say anything.

❧

I stepped out of the chilly little room with the bath in it, shivering in my nightgown. Ariadne came out of the one next door, but she somehow looked a lot better than I did.

"Aren't you cold?" I asked. "Those lukewarm baths are awful."

"Oh, Daddy used to make me take cold baths for my 'health,'" she said disdainfully. "I find these much more pleasant."

I laughed and she grinned.

We headed back to room thirteen. I knocked politely on the door, just in case Scarlet was changing. "Go away," came the muffled voice from within.

Hmmph. Well, if we weren't being polite, so be it. I pushed open the door and went in, Ariadne trailing behind me.

Scarlet was writing something in her new notebook. As soon as she saw us, she shoved it under her sheets.

"Oh, come on," I said. "I'm fed up with all the secrecy." *Hypocrite*, my mind said. *Yes, well*, I told myself. *You can't tell her about Penny for her own good.* "What's going on? Why are you so cross all of a sudden?"

Ariadne peered around me. "What's up, Scarlet?" she asked a bit more diplomatically. "Are you still ill? In your ballet clothes?"

Scarlet finally seemed to give in. "*All right*," she snapped. "But promise you won't tell anyone? I don't want Penny the Slug hearing about this."

"Promise," said Ariadne eagerly.

"Miss Finch was supposed to give me extra ballet lessons, okay?" She looked really embarrassed.

"Why?" I asked. Scarlet had always been so wonderful at ballet, I didn't think she needed extra help.

"Because I didn't think I was good enough," she mumbled at the carpet.

I frowned and sat on my bed. "Why didn't you just tell me?"

"I didn't want anyone knowing," she snapped. "But that's not the problem."

"Then what is?" Ariadne asked, plaiting her damp hair with fumbling fingers. It always made her nervous when Scarlet was angry.

"After I pretended to be sick—sorry—I went down to the ballet studio. All that effort and Miss Finch wasn't even there!" She punched her mattress. "I can't believe she's let me down. I waited and waited. She obviously doesn't care."

"I'm sure she didn't mean to let you down," said Ariadne, trying to be cheerful.

I agreed. "Something important probably came up. Perhaps she had a meeting or a doctor's appointment."

"Hmmph," said Scarlet. "She should've told me."

"It wasn't a proper lesson though," Ariadne pointed out. "And if she came to tell you, wouldn't that mean everyone would know she was tutoring you?" Ariadne was always the wise one.

"I *suppose*," said Scarlet.

"Let's just forget about it and...and...read a nice book or something," my friend said with a smile. "I'm sure she'll explain what happened the next time you see her."

But something about this wasn't sitting right with

me. I didn't know if it was the mysterious things I'd been noticing, or the dark dreams, but I had this gnawing feeling in the pit of my stomach. "There wasn't anything...unusual, was there? In the studio, I mean?"

Scarlet sighed, picking at her bedsheets. "Well, her stool was knocked over. And her stick was on the floor. I thought perhaps she'd hurt herself and gone into the office to sit down, but I knocked and there was no one there."

I wrinkled my nose. "Scarlet, she can't...she can't get up the stairs without her stick, can she? And if she wasn't down there..."

Ariadne's face paled. "Do you think something's happened to her?"

I didn't want to say what was on my mind. "We need to tell someone, just in case. This doesn't feel right."

"No," said Scarlet. "We can't, we..."

"We have to," said Ariadne, suddenly taking charge. She puffed out her chest. "Let's find Mrs. Knight."

Scarlet looked distraught. "I can't say why I was meeting her! Nobody can know about it!"

"Scarlet, this isn't the time to worry about saving your own skin," I said angrily.

"Shhh!" said Ariadne, waving a finger at me. "Shhh, shhh, shhh! No more arguing. If we can't tell Mrs. Knight about Scarlet's extra lessons, we'll have to tell her something else. Why don't we tell her we were all supposed to be meeting Miss Finch, to, um...talk about the ballet? We'll say we were going to paint the scenery or something."

I bit my lip. None of us had an ounce of set-painting talent, but Mrs. Knight didn't know that.

"But I already told her I was sick," said Scarlet. She certainly looked sick now.

"We'll say Ivy and I were the ones looking for her," Ariadne explained. "And you just came back to your room for a rest, and now you feel better. Anyway, won't she be more concerned about what's happened to Miss Finch?"

Of course, that was the important thing. My twin and I would have to put our differences behind us.

"Right," I said, and got shakily back to my feet. "Let's go."

I just hoped we weren't too late.

Chapter Ten

SCARLET

We were too late.

By the time we got down to her office, Mrs. Knight must have already gone home. She lived near the school, but I couldn't say where.

I kicked the door and just about restrained myself from cursing.

"What are we going to do *now*?" Ariadne wailed.

"We could call the police," I said.

Ivy gave me a look that said she thought I was being ridiculous. "How exactly are we going to call them? The offices are locked. And even if we could get to a telephone, what would we say? A teacher's been missing for an hour? They'll laugh at us!"

She was right, and I hated it. Our only hope was to talk to the teachers. But most of them had gone home, with the exception of the few staff that stayed overnight. I swallowed. In the past, that had included Miss Finch, when she'd had nowhere else to go. I tried my hardest not to picture her walking stick lying there in the middle of the floor.

"We can try and tell the matron," I said finally. "But I doubt she'll be any use."

✂

We went to the door of the matron's room, only for her to bustle straight into us in her housecoat.

"Oof! Girls," she said, narrowing her neatly plucked eyebrows. "You're supposed to be getting ready for bed. It's lights-out soon, you know!"

"We know, Miss," said Ivy. "We've got a...problem..."

"If you're here to tell me that Josephine Wilcox has been running laps in the corridor in her swimsuit, I already know. That's what I was just on my way to sort out."

"No!" I said quickly, before she could push past us. "It's Miss Finch. We're worried something's happened to her."

The matron stopped in her tracks and looked down at us—or, more accurately, across, because she wasn't very tall. "Whatever makes you say that? She's gone home to bed, I'm sure."

I glanced at Ariadne, hoping she remembered her part of the plan. She took a deep breath and then gave her explanation without, it seemed, taking another one. "Well, Miss, we were on our way to visit Miss Finch, Miss, because she asked us to, you see, it was about the ballet recital, and we were going to paint the scenery, a lovely castle and some trees, you know, that sort of thing, and so we'd arranged a time to meet her this evening, so we went down there, Miss, and—"

At this point, Ivy had the sense to push Ariadne out of the way before she dropped dead from forgetting how her lungs worked. "Miss Finch wasn't there," she said simply.

"And the lights were all off," I added, "and her...her walking stick was left in the middle of the floor."

The matron was looking at us like we were telling her how to fold laundry.

"I'm sure it's nothing to worry about," she said flatly.

"Miss, you don't understand! She wouldn't just leave her stick! She could barely get down the stairs the other day. Something must have happened to her."

"Perhaps she got a new one," the matron suggested. "Perhaps she got tired and went home early. It's a bit soon to be jumping to conclusions, don't you think?"

"But, Miss—" Ivy pleaded.

There was a *crash* from the other end of the corridor.

"*Miss Wilcox, if you're hurt, you only have yourself to blame!*" the matron screeched, dashing away.

Ivy, Ariadne, and I stood there like lost little children.

"This is hopeless," Ivy said eventually. "We're going to have to wait until morning and find Mrs. Knight."

Ariadne was wobbling again. "Oh dear," she started saying. "Maybe Daddy was right about this school being too dangerous. Whatever are we going to do?"

∾

We barely slept a wink that night. But there wasn't much talking either. I was still angry—at the matron for not believing us, at Mrs. Knight for not being there, and at the world in general. Even more than that, I was afraid. I was scared for Miss Finch...and for myself. And I hated being afraid.

My mind was full of darkness. Dark rooms and dark thoughts. And in my dreams, the shadow returned...

Even when the sun rose and the light broke through the curtains, it wasn't enough to clear my head.

I dragged myself out of bed to the sound of the clanging morning bell, and Ivy and I dressed sleepily, nearly bumping into each other.

"Ivy?" I said, as we adjusted our ties in the mirror.

"Hmm?"

"Can we just agree to never keep things from each other ever again?"

She went a bit quiet, but eventually said, "All right."

I reached out and shook her free hand and smiled.

∾

The first thing we did at breakfast was look for Mrs. Knight. Thankfully, she was there, in her usual position at the Richmond table.

"Miss," I said. "Can we talk to you about something privately? It's really important."

She gestured for us to step outside into the hall with her. I saw Ivy nervously glance around for Ariadne, but she was there at the table too, and she gave us a little wave.

It was a bit quieter out in the corridor, but not much. You could still hear the hubbub from the dining hall, and there was an inescapable smell of porridge in the air.

"What is it, girls?" Mrs. Knight asked.

"It's Miss Finch," Ivy said. "We think something might have happened to her."

We went through the story again, though I made sure to breathe more than Ariadne had. I explained every detail, especially the walking stick and the knocked-over piano stool.

"Oh, *girls*." Mrs. Knight sighed.

I gave Ivy a sideways look.

"It's very...noble of you to worry so much about your teacher. And I'm sure it must have been very alarming for you to find the ballet studio empty like that. But I can tell you, she's perfectly fine."

"Really?" Ivy's face lit up.

"She's at home, resting," said Mrs. Knight. "There was a letter from her on my desk this morning.

She's had to take sudden leave, I'm afraid, due to her leg."

"Oh, thank goodness," said Ivy.

The relief flowed through me, but there was a flame of uncertainty still flickering. "What about her walking stick though, Miss? Why would she leave it?"

Mrs. Knight looked puzzled. "I don't know, Scarlet, but it's probably not the only one she owned. Perhaps someone else helped her up the stairs. She's safe, that's what matters."

I nodded.

"Try not to let your imaginations run away with you, girls," she continued. "There's really nothing to worry about now."

"All right," I said. "I mean...yes, Miss."

"Come on then." She plastered on a cheery grin. "Back to breakfast. You must be starving after all that worrying."

I was, but starving enough to enjoy Rookwood porridge? *Blech.*

Chapter Eleven

IVY

As soon as we sat down at our table, Ariadne spoke up. "Miss Jones is back today!"

"Really?" I'd almost forgotten about Miss Jones and how we'd been planning to ask her about our mother.

"I woke up early," Ariadne explained, "and I decided to go to the library. I'd already read the six books I was allowed to take out this week, but I thought I'd be sneaky and ask for an extra one to have before Monday."

She blushed and I smiled, thinking how that was a very Ariadne thing to do. I'd missed her funny ways.

Scarlet's expression had been mostly thunderous all morning, but now the clouds cleared. "Finally," she said, a glint in her eye.

After clearing away our breakfast trays, we raced to the library. It was Saturday, so we had no classes to go to.

Miss Jones looked a good deal better than the last time I'd seen her, which had been shortly after the fire and the arrest of Mr. Bartholomew. His arrest had been partially thanks to crucial evidence that she'd remembered from her own school days at Rookwood, and it was that which made me think she might well be able to help us now.

She was making notes on a small pad, but she closed it as we approached. It said "Catastrophe" on the cover: her first name, strange as it might seem.

She pushed a strand of jet-black hair behind her ear. "Morning, girls. Ariadne, I have to say, if you're here for another book, I think that might be somewhat pushing it."

"No, Miss," said Ariadne sheepishly.

"It's research, really," said Scarlet. "About Rookwood's past. Hunting a ghost."

The librarian's face went a little pale. "Oh. Well..." she said quietly, looking down at her desk.

"Don't worry, Miss," I said quickly. "It won't be about anything distressing. Well, mostly not. I hope." The librarian had been distraught when she'd realized that she'd seen the headmaster on the day of

Emmeline Adel's murder. "It's just about the time that you went here, and the girls you attended with."

"Is that so? Well, I'm sure I could spare a little time to talk about it." She smiled bravely at me. "I know that the things you girls get up to have a tendency to be rather...important."

Scarlet grinned like a Cheshire cat, and Ariadne looked like she'd just been given a medal.

"Come on, then. I'll just get someone to man—or should I say woman?—the desk. Anna?" she called into the stacks.

Anna Santos appeared with a pile of books. She was one of the oldest girls in our year, born in September (Scarlet and I were the youngest, having come into the world rather late on the last day of August). She was tall and pretty, with tanned skin and perfectly curled brown hair. "Here, Miss," she said.

"Can you watch the desk for a bit, please?"

Anna looked flustered. "What do I do if somebody comes?"

"Just as I told you," said Miss Jones. "You fill in their name, what book they've taken out, and how many they're allowed to borrow the rest of the week. Come on, you know this!"

"Oh. Well. Yes," Anna replied. A seventh grader approached the desk as we walked away. "Name!" Anna demanded like an army drill officer.

"She's a bit cold, that one," Miss Jones whispered. Coming from someone who had "Catastrophe" embroidered on her handkerchief, I wasn't sure it meant much.

We perched on the window seat at the back of the library, in the same spot where we'd spoken last term and decades-old secrets had come spilling out. I almost hoped there was some magic to it, and that the librarian would once again have something important to tell us.

"So," said Miss Jones, "what was it you girls wanted to ask about?"

Scarlet took a deep breath. "It's about our mother, Miss."

"Not my mother," said Ariadne helpfully, "theirs." She pointed at me and Scarlet.

"We barely knew her," said Scarlet, "but we did know her name. Which was, well, we thought... Emmeline Adel."

Miss Jones blinked rapidly. "Oh...oh no...the poor girl from the lake..." Her face crumpled, and I worried that she was going to cry again, but she held herself together.

"But that's just it," I said. "Our mother couldn't have been *Emmeline*, could she? Emmeline died when she was just a girl. So we think, whoever our mother was, she took Emmeline's identity for some reason."

"And you think your mother was one of the students here too?" Miss Jones asked.

We nodded.

The librarian bit her lip and studied the floor. "I'm sorry, girls, but I'm not sure I can help you."

"What?" said Scarlet, ever tactful. "Why?"

"I wasn't here for very long, you see. And I spent most of my time with my nose in a book. I remember a few names, or a few faces, but seldom both." We all must have looked so disappointed that she started to rack her brains. "I mean...perhaps...hmm..."

"Can you not remember *anything* else, Miss?" Ariadne asked.

"I think," she replied, "that I might still have the school photograph from one of the years I attended. Would that be of interest?"

I looked at the others. It certainly would. "Yes! Please, Miss."

"All right," she said. "I'll do my best to dig it up. It's probably at my parents' house, so you might have to wait until next week."

"Thank you, Miss," I replied with a grin.

We left the library with the wind back in our sails. Our mother might be in that photograph, and then maybe we would be closer to knowing who she really was. Perhaps the shadowy figure in my dreams would finally show her face.

Chapter Twelve

SCARLET

The last thing I expected to do on Monday was to meet the new ballet teacher.

Usually if Miss Finch was ill, she was only gone for a day, and we'd just have to do some work on our own or go to one of the other sports classes. This meant Miss Finch was truly gone, at least for a while.

Ivy and I walked into class with all the other girls and saw a complete stranger standing in front of Miss Finch's piano.

She was a slim, elegant woman. She was dressed all in white, even up to her hair, which was a starry, silvery white itself, and it was tied back in a tight bun. But she wasn't old; in fact, she didn't look much older than Miss Finch. She was beautiful and glamorous, but in a...sharp way. Like a knife.

"Line up at the back of the room, girls," she said.

She spoke with a hint of an accent, and something in there practically commanded you to listen.

With a nervous glance at Ivy, I fell into line. Who was this woman?

As if she'd read my mind, she announced, "My name is Madame Grizelda Gates. You will call me Madame Zelda."

I looked around the class. They all seemed as shocked as I was.

Madame Zelda put an exaggerated hand to her ear. "Excuse me?"

"Yes, Miss," we chorused.

She started walking up and down the line, looking at each of us in turn. "Welcome to my class, girls. I assure you, any misbehavior will not be tolerated. You may find my methods...unusual. But I expect the best. And I will get the best. Understood?"

"Yes, Miss!"

"Now," she said. "You watch."

She danced without music. She just began.

I watched with my mouth hanging open. She danced like a real prima ballerina. Like a star. This was what I wanted to do. This was what I wanted to *be*.

And as I thought that, I felt my heart fill up with guilt. Miss Finch may not have been able to dance this way anymore, but she was still a great teacher, and she'd saved my life. Now this strange woman had showed up, and it was like she was weaving some kind of evil enchantment.

She danced *en pointe* like it was nothing, barely showing the strain. Sometimes she leaped and sprang, sometimes her movements were slow and graceful. But it was all perfect.

When she had finished the dance, we stood there, speechless. Eventually, Nadia started to clap. Then we were all applauding.

There was the barest flicker of a smile on the new teacher's face. "That is what *you* can do. With dedication, and practice, practice, practice." She tapped out each *practice* with her toe on the hard floor. "Now—warm up."

We dutifully went over to the *barre* and began.

"Miss," Penny piped up. "How did you—"

Madame Zelda shot a look at her. "This is not the time for talking."

"Sorry, Miss!" Penny actually looked a bit terrified, and I stifled a giggle.

"What's your name, girl?" the teacher demanded.

"Penny Winchester, Miss."

"In my class, you will be silent, and you will listen. Listen to me and to the music. If you have any questions, you may talk at the end."

I watched Penny struggle as she tried to decide whether this warranted a "Yes, Miss," or if that counted as talking. In the end, she just settled for a nod and joined us at the *barre*. Ha!

Madame Zelda's eyes seemed to follow you around the room. She insisted on demonstrating everything, and if you so much as looked anywhere else she'd stop and stare you down until she was sure you were paying attention again.

I was trying to perfect my *arabesque*, one leg raised high behind me, and I *felt* her looking at me. Of course, that made me wobble. "Start again," she ordered.

I wanted to whisper to Ivy, but I didn't want any more commands from that strange voice, so I stayed quiet. My twin gave me a worried look.

Would Madame Zelda have horrible punishments up her sleeve for disobedient girls? Mrs. Knight had tried to put an end to all that, but...I didn't want to find out.

By the end of the class, we were exhausted. I'd barely had time to worry about whether or not I was doing my best.

Madame Zelda had us all line up again for *reverence*, where we bowed and curtseyed to slow music. Her piano playing was almost as good as her dancing, but seeing her at Miss Finch's piano gave me chills. It was *wrong*, somehow.

"Thank you, girls," she said finally. "Next time, you will do better." She waved us away with an elegant hand, and then disappeared into the back room.

I exhaled with relief—in fact, I think the whole class did.

"Well, that was strange," Nadia said quietly.

I noticed everyone was unlacing their shoes a bit quicker than usual.

When Ivy and I reached the top of the stairs, we didn't head straight for our room. Instead we just stood in the corridor, watching everyone go past.

"What the heck just happened?" I said. "Where did *she* come from?"

Ivy rubbed her forehead nervously and shrugged.

I couldn't shake that air of *wrongness*, and I was beginning to realize why. "If Miss Finch has only been gone for a weekend," I said, "how did they recruit a new teacher so quickly? And how come she wasn't even mentioned in assembly this morning?"

"It's fishy," Ivy said.

"More than fishy. It's like a whole shark. And I want to know why," I said.

∞

Not long after, I knocked on the door of Mrs. Knight's office and shoved it open.

"Oh, hello, girls," Mrs. Knight pushed her reading glasses up on her nose. "Is something the matter?"

"Can we talk to you about something, Miss?" I asked.

Mrs. Knight looked down at her watch. "I've got a few minutes. Come inside."

Our interim headmistress had taken over Mr. Bartholomew's office, which had been dark, dreary, and filled with heavy furniture. She seemed to have given it quite a makeover, and now it looked almost *jolly*.

The walls were now painted a shade of pale pink,

and she'd added motivational posters everywhere with slogans like "Win your way with a smile!" and "Today is the day for a fresh start!"

"Sit down, girls," Mrs. Knight said, gesturing at the two chairs that faced her desk. "Now, what was it you wanted to talk about?"

"Well, we had our ballet class this afternoon, Miss..." Ivy started.

"Ah." The teacher took her glasses off. "You've met Madame Zelda then? We were most impressed by her résumé. And doesn't she dance like a dream?"

"She's amazing, Miss," I agreed.

"I'm sure the recital will be wonderful with her on board. Anyway, was there a problem?"

"We were just..." Ivy was stumbling. I could tell she'd realized that maybe it was a little inappropriate for us to be questioning the acting headmistress about a teacher she'd hired.

Luckily for Ivy, "inappropriate" is practically my middle name. "It's weird, Miss. *She's* weird. And how did you manage to find someone to fill in so quickly?"

My twin frowned at me. "Oh well," Mrs. Knight said, waving her hand dismissively. "Her application arrived shortly after Miss Finch went on sick leave."

That sounded even more suspicious. "How did she know that Miss Finch was gone?"

"She didn't," said Mrs. Knight. "Just a happy coincidence." There was a big heap of paperwork on her desk, and she'd started flicking through it absentmindedly.

I looked at Ivy. More like an *unhappy* coincidence. I didn't trust Madame Zelda at all. Why would she have even applied, when Rookwood already had a ballet teacher?

"Have you heard from Miss Finch, Miss?"

"Hmm…what? Oh, no. Just the letter she wrote. Nothing since then." She reached into her tray and pulled out a piece of paper, and handed it to me. "Is that all, girls? I've got something important to fill out."

I looked down at the paper fleetingly. It was in Miss Finch's handwriting.

Hello to all at Rookwood. I expect you've been worried. I've been forced to take leave suddenly due to my injured leg getting worse. Please understand that this was unfortunately beyond my control. Rest assured that I will make every effort to come back when I'm recovered.

Kind regards,
Rebecca Finch

I breathed a sigh of relief. Mrs. Knight had already started filling out her form and didn't ask for the letter back, so I kept hold of it.

"Thank you for your time, Miss," said Ivy.

Miss Finch really *was* fine. We were worrying for nothing.

So why couldn't I shake the feeling that we were missing something?

Chapter Thirteen

IVY

Meeting the new ballet teacher was strange. But at least I felt reassured that Miss Finch was all right. Perhaps Madame Zelda was nothing more than a little eccentric.

We headed for dinner, feeling a little calmer.

Ariadne was already tucking into her stew. For some reason she had asked for an extra helping. The dinner lady had looked so shocked that she'd just agreed.

"There's this new ballet teacher," said Scarlet to Ariadne. "I think she came from the moon."

"Really? Why?" said Ariadne.

"She has these weird eyes," said Scarlet, waving her finger in circles. "And silvery white hair. And she talks funny."

Penny suddenly leaned over. "I'll tell her you said that, shall I?" she said with gleeful malice.

Scarlet did a great job of looking as though she

wasn't bothered. "Go ahead. It won't make you a better dancer than me, will it?"

Penny made a noise like "ugh" and sat down in her seat heavily, her tray hitting the table and stew sloshing over the sides of her plate.

"I want to meet her," said Ariadne, carrying on as if the interruption had never happened. "She sounds interesting."

We carried on eating our dinner and talking about the strange new addition to the teaching staff.

While Ariadne and Scarlet were still chatting, I headed over to drop off my plate with the dirty dishes. I was just scraping off some of the leftovers when someone whispered in my ear. "You ought to tell your sister to watch her tongue."

I jumped. Penny was at my back again, flanked by Josephine and Clara. "Go away," I said. I was trying to sound nonchalant, but I realized I was holding my plate up like a shield.

"Worried I'm going to tip your dinner over you again?" Penny asked, smirking. "No need. I have better ideas this time." She tapped her freckled nose. Her friends giggled.

Perhaps if I said nothing, she'd just give up and go away.

"I *will* get Scarlet kicked out, whatever it takes," Penny continued, pinching my wrist cruelly. "I wonder how long it'll take before you give in and tell her?"

I looked desperately for Scarlet and Ariadne, but

they were engrossed in conversation and the hall was in uproar as always. "Let go!" I squeaked.

Penny glanced around, and then swiftly kicked me in the leg as she loosened her grip.

"Ow!" I cried.

Just at that moment, Nadia's older sister Meena walked past. She frowned. "Are these girls giving you trouble, Ivy?"

Penny blinked, as if she had no idea what had just happened. "Oh, I must have slipped," she said with a nauseating smile.

"You kicked me!" I said.

"Penny wouldn't do such a thing," Josephine said. "She's a prefect, after all." Clara winked at me, and they all walked away. *Ugh.* I slammed my plate down on the counter.

"Ignore them," Meena said. "They're nothing but trouble. I'm just glad Nadia isn't so swayed by them anymore."

"Me too," I said, breathing a sigh of relief. "Thank you, Meena."

Whatever it takes... I really didn't like the sound of that. I'd seen how far Penny could go.

We headed back to our room, and Scarlet sat down on her bed. As she did so, Miss Finch's letter fell out of her pocket.

"What's that?" Ariadne asked.

My twin looked down at it. "Oh. We went to talk to Mrs. Knight again. She gave me this letter from Miss Finch."

"Can I see?" said Ariadne. She walked over and picked it up.

Moments later, she dropped it, her face turning pale.

"What's wrong?" I asked.

She pointed shakily at the note. "Look at the first letter of each line."

I did as she said as Ariadne continued. "And why has she written it down the middle of the page like that? And why not address it formally to Mrs. Knight?"

"Oh no! Oh no..." I put my hand over my mouth, horrified. "Surely not..." But it was there on the page, plain as day.

"What?" Scarlet exclaimed. "What are you talking about?"

"It says *'help me'*!" Ariadne cried. "Oh my gosh! Poor Miss Finch! What on earth could have happened?"

Scarlet grabbed the letter and reread it, her eyes burning with intensity. "How did I miss this?"

"We need to tell Mrs. Knight," said Ariadne, nervously wringing her hands. "She'll surely telephone the police, won't she?"

"She'll have to do something," said Scarlet.

And this time I felt sure that my twin was right.

❧

We ran back downstairs, passing the matron in the corridor.

"*Girls!*" she yelled after us. "Slow down!"

"No time! Important!" Scarlet called back over her shoulder. We thundered down the stairs and along the hallway until we came to Mrs. Knight's office. She was standing outside it, just locking the door for the night.

"Miss," said Scarlet, tugging on her arm. "You really need to see this."

"Can it wait, Miss Gray?" retorted Mrs. Knight.

"It absolutely can't," Scarlet declared.

Mrs. Knight turned around impatiently, tucking the office key into her pocket.

"This note," Scarlet held it out, "that Miss Finch left you. Didn't you read it? Look at the first letter of each line!"

"Miss Gray," chastised Mrs. Knight, "a little respect for your elders, please!"

Scarlet wasn't listening. "Look!" she said, tapping the paper.

Mrs. Knight sighed and pulled her glasses down from the top of her head. She stared at the note, and I thought I saw a momentary flicker of worry pass over her face. "Oh, girls," she said a little wretchedly. "You really have vivid imaginations. It's just a coincidence."

"A coincidence?" said Ariadne, and we all turned to look at her. "It's a cry for help, Miss, can't you see?"

"Not you too, Ariadne dear," Mrs. Knight groaned. "You're usually so *sensible*." She plucked the note from Scarlet's grasp, folded it up and placed it in her pocket in a decisive manner. "For the last time, there is nothing wrong with Miss Finch. I spoke to her on the telephone myself not ten minutes ago. The school is safe now, do you hear? How many times must I repeat myself?"

"Really?" Scarlet asked. "You spoke to her?"

Mrs. Knight looked as though she was about to start shouting.

"She is *fine*, Miss Gray. She simply said she won't be back for some time. Now, can we please forget about this nonsense and go off to our beds, as we are *supposed* to be doing?"

We all looked at each other in defeat.

Ariadne gave in first. "Yes, Miss," she said. She quickly side-eyed Scarlet and me.

"Yes, Miss," we chorused.

That evening, I felt like I was on a seesaw. One minute I'd tell myself that everything was fine, that nothing was going to happen, that Miss Finch wasn't in a bit of danger. And the next I'd hear a sudden noise, or a draft would blow the curtains around, and everything would come rushing back. I had no idea what was real and what was imagined.

"Do you think Miss Finch is really safe?" I asked Scarlet.

She yawned. "I'm not convinced."

I paused as I pulled my nightgown on. "Do you think *we're* safe? I mean, all these things that keep happening. Could it not be...Miss Fo—"

"No," said Scarlet firmly. "Don't even think it. *She's* gone. Madame Zelda though... I don't trust her."

I said nothing. Scarlet didn't even want to consider the possibility, and honestly, neither did I.

We shared a look. "Let's push the desk in front of the door, just in case," she suggested. Together we hauled the heavy desk over so it blocked the doorway.

That night my dreams came back more vividly than ever. I was on that hilltop again, with the shadow out in front of me. She still wouldn't turn around, no matter how much I screamed.

I woke for a few moments, and when I slipped back under the dream changed.

I was in my bed, and I felt as though I was still asleep. But as I tried to move, I was trapped, my blankets pinning me down.

And as I lay there, bathed in moonlight, I saw a shadow pass under the door.

Who was it? Our mother? Or someone...else?

I tried to call out, but my voice made no sound.

All I could do was stare as an eye appeared at the keyhole, watching...waiting... Then the doorknob turned.

I held my breath.

The door creaked open, the heavy desk in front of it melting away into thin air. And the shadow came into our room. A woman. It flowed toward me, and in words that were like the rustling of the wind in the trees, it whispered: "Ivy..."

✀

I jumped awake. My heart was pounding and my palms sweating. I looked over at the door, but there was nothing there. The desk hadn't moved an inch.

Just a dream, I told myself as I trembled under the covers.

Eventually, I drifted back off to sleep.

✀

The bright sun lit the room, and I slowly woke up. I immediately felt better. It was always harder to be scared on a sunny morning. There was no one coming for us. Miss Finch was safe. I had to believe that. Perhaps everything really was all right.

Or at least, so I thought, until I walked into English class a few minutes early, and I saw the blackboard.

And I screamed.

Chapter Fourteen

SCARLET

I was a little way behind Ivy, chatting to Dot Campbell, when I heard the scream. Then I ran.

I almost slammed right into the back of her. She was standing just inside the door of the classroom, her hand over her mouth. She'd gone completely white.

"Ivy, what—" I asked.

She just pointed at the blackboard.

NO ONE IS SAFE

It was written in huge letters, scrawled across the entire board.

I felt the world spin under me. *It was her. She's back.* All I could think of was that night on the roof, being dragged away, the walls of the asylum pressing in...

"Oh my word!"

That outburst snapped me back to reality. It was Dot, who had just walked in. "Who...who wrote that?" she asked, her voice wobbling.

Neither of us could speak. My twin couldn't take her eyes off the words.

More girls began to pour in. That was when the whispers started.

"It's a prank," I heard someone say.

"Is it part of the lesson?"

"Who wrote it?"

"There's that weird new girl..."

"Does someone want to hurt us?"

"I am writing this in my prefect book right away!" cried a shrill voice. That was Penny, of course.

I could hear Ivy's panicked breathing beginning to slow.

Pull yourself together, Scarlet. It's just a prank. Writing can't hurt you.

"I'm fine," I said to nobody in particular, but I gripped Ivy's arm and didn't let go.

I heard a frightened gasp right by my ear. "Oh gosh," Ariadne whispered.

"Class, what is the meaning of this?"

Miss Charlett had finally entered the room, and she was looking at the board in bewilderment.

"You mean you didn't write it, Miss?" Dot asked nervously.

Well, duh, I wanted to say. I didn't think there were

any famous pieces of literature that went by the name of *No One Is Safe*.

Miss Charlett snapped her head back and forth furiously. "Was this one of you, girls?"

"No, Miss!" everyone insisted at once.

She darted over to the board and began frantically rubbing away the writing with the eraser. A big gray smudge formed as the words disappeared. But they were burned into my mind.

The teacher turned to us, hands on her hips. She looked anxious and angry all at the same time. "Mrs. Knight is going to hear about this. If any of you were responsible..." She breathed out. "Let's just calm down and get on with the lesson, shall we?"

I took my seat next to Ivy. There was a strong smell of chalk dust in the air.

"Just a nasty prank," Miss Charlett said firmly. "Nothing more."

∝

The class passed in a blur. As I staggered out into the hallway, I heard everyone burst into discussion of the message.

Ariadne blinked up at me, wide-eyed and mousy again. "Who do you think could have written it?" she asked. She was gripping her satchel so tightly it looked like her books were about to explode out of it at any moment.

"You don't think..." said Ivy, her voice so quiet it was almost a whisper. "It could be...?"

I stopped in my tracks. "Who?"

"*You know who*," she replied. There was fear in her eyes.

"No," I said quickly. "No. She's long gone, I told you. It's just someone messing around."

Ariadne gulped. "Who then?"

"I don't know," I said. I started to walk in the direction of our next class, Ivy and Ariadne scuttling along in my wake. It *had* to be someone else. But for a second, staring up at that board, I'd thought it too.

"Well, don't Penny and Violet have a habit of writing horrible things on blackboards?" Ivy pointed out.

That was sort of true. Back in seventh grade they had drawn a hideous caricature of me, looking like I was dead, all crossed eyes and stuck-out tongue. "It's not their style," I said. "Besides, Penny is too busy being Miss Perfect Prefect these days, and Violet only cares about Rose."

It was funny that I chose to mention Rose at that exact moment. As we passed the back door of the school, we noticed a huge commotion coming from outside.

"What the—?" Ivy muttered. All three of us leaned out of the door. There was a group of older girls in jodhpurs and riding helmets pointing and yelling at each other, then running toward the stables.

I dashed outside, into the drizzle, and off down the path.

"Wait!" Ivy called after me. "Scarlet!"

"We'll be late for biology!" Ariadne wailed.

I ignored them, feeling the gravel crunch under my feet as I ran. I heard their footsteps catching up with me.

We reached the stables, where the commotion was even bigger.

And there, standing in the middle of all of it, was Rose.

She was shrinking back against the big tree in the middle of the stable yard, and she looked utterly terrified.

"What did you *do*?" an older girl demanded. It was Pansy Jenson, a prefect from the eleventh grade—tall and pretty, but with an irritatingly posh voice. She prodded Rose in the chest. "Answer me!"

Rose bit her lip. There were tears on her cheeks.

Everyone started shouting again, until it was all just a blur of noise. Ivy grabbed my arm, but it was too late. I could feel the burning inside my chest.

"*Leave her alone!*" I yelled. I barreled through the horsey girls until I was right by Rose. I stood in front of her like a shield, my arms folded. "What the heck is going on?"

"Get out of the way, you little fool!" Pansy sneered. "She needs to answer for what she's done!"

She tried to push past me, so I kicked her swiftly in one jodhpur-clad leg.

"Ow! You beast!" She clutched at her shin and hopped backward.

"Stay away from Rose," I ordered. Ivy and Ariadne had managed to push their way through to the front and were staring at me in horror. "What do you think she's done?"

"Look around you!" Pansy waved her long arms about.

I turned my head slowly, and saw to my surprise that every stable door was wide open. *Every single one.* And not a horse in sight.

"Someone turned the horses loose?" Ariadne asked, dismayed.

"Not *someone*," said one of Pansy's snooty friends. "This *freak*." She pointed an accusing finger at Rose, who was clinging on to the back of my dress.

"Rose wouldn't do that," I insisted. "She loves ponies more than *anything*. You've got it wrong."

Pansy glared down her nose at me, her nostrils flaring. "She was the only one here. And it wasn't any of *us*, was it, girls?"

She looked around at all the other identical riding girls, who were shaking their heads aggressively. "Where did she even come from?" the blond one scoffed. "She's not even a real student, is she? She's just some strange girl who turned up one day, and they let her look after our horses! It's not right!"

I pointed at her. "If you don't shut up, I'll kick you as well."

"You violent little..." she started.

Ivy darted forward. The older girls all looked back and forth between her and me. "Everyone just calm down," she said. "Scarlet's telling the truth. Rose wouldn't do this."

"Then why doesn't she defend herself?" Pansy demanded. "She just stands there crying and looking stupid!"

"She's crying because you're yelling at her, you idiot!" I shouted back. "And she doesn't talk to people she doesn't *trust*. So, she's not going to talk to a vile slug like you, is she?"

"Well, I never!" said Pansy.

Ivy linked her arm through mine. "Please, we'll sort this out. She'll talk to us." She frowned at the assembled crowd. "Why don't you go and tell Mrs. Knight about your horses instead of attacking an innocent person?"

"And if you want to get to Rose," I added, "you'll have to go through us first."

"And me!" Ariadne said, leaping forward and attaching herself to Ivy's arm so that there was a little chain of us.

Pansy bared her teeth at me, looking a little like a horse herself. "Fine," she growled. "But if she's responsible..."

"Leave it, Pansy," her friend said, dragging her away. The gaggle of other girls trotted away behind them, talking loudly.

When my breathing had finally slowed back down to normal, I dropped Ivy's arm.

"Are you all right, Rose?" Ivy asked.

Rose nodded, but her tears said otherwise.

"Who did this?" Ariadne's voice was high-pitched.

Rose shook her head and waved her hands, as if to say, *I have no idea.*

I looked around at the stable doors. Some of the bolts had been wrenched clean off, leaving both the upper and lower parts of doors swinging as if they'd been thrown open without even a thought.

Ivy suddenly went pale. "Scarlet…" She pointed at one of the doors. "That one's different," she said. I followed her finger. The bolt had been carefully slid back, the door neatly fixed in place.

And I knew, without even having to look, that the nameplate above it would be a single word.

Raven.

Chapter Fifteen

IVY

It took us some time to calm Rose down, sitting in the straw under the tree as the rain dripped around us. When she finally said a few words, we realized she was actually even more distraught about the whereabouts of the horses than she was about the mean girls. "I can't find them," she whispered, another tear rolling down her cheek.

"Well, there's one over there," said Ariadne, pointing. A rather fat pony was standing in one of the flower beds, chewing on what looked like a particularly luxurious plant.

Then Ariadne launched into the story of how she'd lost her pony, Oswald, who had been lured away by boys with sweets, until Rose was giggling through her tears.

"Mrs. Knight will be here soon," I said. "She'll send everyone off to look for them, I'm sure."

Ariadne went a bit pale. "Oh gosh, I hope we don't get a detention for missing biology! That would be frightful!"

"Ariadne," Scarlet said, eyes narrowed. "You need to get your priorities straight."

Ariadne's expression didn't change. "Detention," she muttered, as if that were the most horrifying thing that could happen.

Scarlet was strangely silent, her fists balled up. I'd expected her to keep ranting about the horsey girls and their awful behavior, but for some reason she didn't seem to have the words.

"Scarlet," I said tentatively, "what about Raven's stall?"

"It doesn't mean anything," Scarlet protested. "Anyone could've done this."

I really wasn't so sure. Miss Fox's raven-black horse, the threat on the blackboard... I rubbed my arms as a chill passed over me.

Miss Fox. The terrible headmistress. She had taken my sister from me. What if the shadowy figure in my dreams wasn't our mother—what if it was *her*!

"Scarlet, I really think—"

My sister interrupted me. "It must be someone else," she said, as if that were final.

Eventually, we heard crunching footsteps and Mrs. Knight appeared, alongside Miss Bowler, the swimming teacher. Beside them in a tall hat was Miss

Linton, who taught horseback riding. I rarely saw her around the school, presumably because she was always out riding.

"What's going on?" boomed Miss Bowler.

Miss Linton was clutching her riding crop. "The horses!" she cried, seeing the state of the stable doors. "Oh, Rose, whatever did you do?"

"It wasn't Rose!" Scarlet yelled, jumping to her feet. "Those trolls only think it was her because they don't know a thing about her!"

"She wouldn't do this, Miss." I scrambled up and brushed the straw from my dress. I felt certain that Miss Linton would know how much Rose cared for the horses.

"Hmm," was all Miss Linton would say, her lower lip wobbling as she glanced around. Many of the horses and ponies were paid for by rich parents—if anything had happened to them, she would be in big trouble.

"That girl is a liability!" Miss Bowler bellowed. "I'm not sure why we've got her on school property at all..."

"*Really*, Eunice!" Mrs. Knight suddenly said. "This is not the time." She turned to us, leaving Miss Bowler dumbstruck. "Girls, get back to your lessons immediately. And no more fighting, do you hear me?"

"But, Miss," Scarlet started, "there's something you should—"

"Enough!" I'd never seen Mrs. Knight so stern. "In, *now!*"

"Yes, Miss," we chorused.

Rose pointed at herself, wordlessly.

"Yes, you too," Mrs. Knight added.

Scarlet made an *ugh* sound, then pushed past the teachers and out of the yard.

∞

Together we headed back toward the school. The drizzle was easing off, turning into a fine mist.

I was cold and sad and afraid. And my mood wasn't much improved when we met Violet coming the other way. She looked furious.

"Rose!" she cried. "Are you all right?"

Rose nodded. She was clinging on to Ariadne's arm, her eyes still red from crying.

Violet's dark hair was sticking up in the rain. "I heard people saying the horses were gone and that you'd let them escape. Did they hurt you? I'll *kill* them!"

I couldn't help noticing that Scarlet shuddered. She had never forgotten Violet's dark side.

"We protected her," said Ariadne fiercely. Rose nodded.

"It should have been me," said Violet, through gritted teeth. "*I'm* your friend."

Rose looked around, wide-eyed. I think she was thinking that we were all her friends—or at least, I hoped so.

"We haven't got time for this," said Scarlet, glaring at Violet. She turned and dashed off toward the school door. Which was strange—I didn't think Scarlet would be in a hurry to return to class.

As Rose took Violet's hand, I smiled apologetically and ran off after Scarlet.

I caught up with her in the hallway. She was leaning against one of the big windows, her face wrought with worry.

"What is it?" I asked. "Is it Violet?"

My twin narrowed her eyes. "Violet isn't the problem. We need to know who's behind this."

"Scarlet," I pleaded. "I really think that Miss Fox could be involved. I've been having these dreams, and—"

Her face contorted. "No," she snapped viciously. "I don't want to hear that name *ever again*." She paused, looking uncertain for a moment. "Dreams don't mean anything."

I leaned against the window next to my twin, the glass cold and damp under my nose. No matter what she said, I couldn't help looking around, just to make sure we were alone.

My worries were interrupted as Ariadne appeared, trotting along the corridor. She was huffing and puffing, her mousy hair displaying copious amounts of frizz from the drizzle. "You're too fast for me!" she wheezed. "What did I miss?"

Scarlet spoke before I could. "Ivy thinks you-know-who might be back," she said with derision. "Which is clearly impossible."

"What I don't understand," Ariadne continued,

straightening up, "is how she could be doing all this…
if it is her, I mean. And why she'd risk coming back to
the school. She knows the police are after her!"

"Exactly! So, what if it's someone else?" said Scarlet
suddenly. I knew from the expression on her face that
an idea had gripped her.

"Who?" asked Ariadne, looking around quickly. She
even looked down at herself momentarily, as if she
might be a suspect.

Scarlet snapped her fingers and both of us jumped.
"Madame Zelda. That new ballet teacher who just conve-
niently turned up when all these strange things began
happening. I *keep* telling everyone that she's suspicious."

"But Mrs. Knight said—" I started.

"Mrs. Knight doesn't know what she's talking
about!" Scarlet snapped. "Madame Zelda is involved
somehow, I *know it*!"

"Maybe you're right," I said.

"Of course, I am!" Scarlet said. "And if we can
prove she's involved, perhaps everyone will stop
picking on Rose…"

"*Girls!*" Miss Bowler's bellow echoed down the
corridor. I gulped as she pounded toward us. "Right!
You've missed enough lessons already. Get to class
immediately!"

"But, Miss—" Scarlet protested.

"Do you not value your education, Miss Gray? Do
all of you want to write me an essay on the subject?"
the swimming teacher demanded.

"No thanks, Miss," Scarlet replied.

Miss Bowler picked up Scarlet's satchel and shoved it into her arms. "Right then. *Class!*"

We hurried away in silence, Ariadne clutching my arm in fear. I almost laughed. There were far worse things to be afraid of than Miss Bowler.

Chapter Sixteen

SCARLET

The whispers about Rose were everywhere. Those horsey know-it-alls had seen to that.

It used to be me that everyone whispered about. Now there was a new target, and there was nothing gossipy girls liked better. The rumors followed us through class and along the corridors.

"That strange new girl who never talks. I heard she let all the horses loose. Can you believe it?"

"I heard she's deaf *and* dumb."

"They shouldn't have let her stay in our school..."

"I heard she escaped from an insane asylum!"

I nearly punched the person who said that last one.

Rose and Violet were missing from dinner, as were Mrs. Knight and some of the other teachers. That only caused more rumors to fly.

"I do hope Rose hasn't been punished," Ariadne said. She was staring mournfully at her plate.

"She'd better not have been," I said darkly. "Or I'll let them have a piece of my mind."

Ivy gave me a withering look. "No, you won't," she said. "We don't need you getting all of us in trouble. Again."

"All right, all right, fine. No trouble," I grumbled.

"And Miss Jones might be back tomorrow," Ivy added.

That was true. My cold heart thawed a little at the idea of her bringing the picture of our mother. At least there was something good in the world.

After a chilly bath that evening, I shivered in my threadbare towel, teeth chattering. Ivy came out of the bathroom next door in a similar state. We quickly dashed back to room thirteen and pulled our nightgowns on.

The matron tossed a half-hearted "Lights out, girls," through the door as we dived under the covers. We had to wait until she was gone before heaving the heavy desk back into its guarding position.

"Do you think it's enough?" Ivy asked, climbing back into her bed again.

I knew what she meant. *Enough to keep us safe from whoever was out there.* "Let's just pray it is."

I settled down in bed, but I swore for a second I heard heels clicking down the corridor.

And it wasn't long after that we heard the scream.

✺

You should probably run *away* from a scream. But nobody does. You always want to find out what caused it.

I'd jumped up before Ivy, and started dragging at the desk. She stumbled over to help, then I tugged open the door and peered out.

Other girls were already staring down the corridor. The window at the far end was wide open, the thin curtains blowing in the breeze. I saw Clara Brand standing near it, her eyes wide with horror.

"*Help!*" she started yelling. "Help! It's Josephine! She's fallen!"

Penny stepped out, blinking and rubbing her eyes in the semi-darkness. "*Fallen?* Out of the *window?*"

Clara nodded and began crying hysterically.

"Someone get the nurse!" Penny yelled. "And someone get the matron! *Quick!*"

I looked at Ivy. We weren't far from the matron's room. I ran, and she followed. I saw Nadia dashing off in the direction of Nurse Gladys's office as the others thundered downstairs in their nightgowns.

I hammered on the matron's door, and it wasn't long before she appeared, yawning. She had a pair of fluffy earmuffs on over her hair rollers.

"Miss, please," Ivy said desperately, "come quick. Josephine's fallen out of the window."

The matron's face went from baffled sleepiness

to complete shock. "Oh, dear Lord," she whispered. "Right, right, oh goodness." She picked up a flashlight with a large handle and her travel bag and kept on muttering horrified nonsense as we half-dragged her down the stairs.

What was beneath that window? I didn't want to think the worst. Josephine was one of Penny's horrible sidekicks, and I'd never liked her, but that didn't mean I wanted her to *die.*

We made it to the ground floor just as Nadia appeared with the nurse. None of us could speak.

The matron was still babbling. "I *told* her not to play in the corridor, and I told her to stop messing around with that window, the stupid, stupid girl..."

The front door of the school was wide open to the darkness beyond. The others must have already run outside. But why was the door unlocked...?

We dashed out into the cold, with no coats or shoes. The gravel of the driveway tore holes in the stockings we wore to bed. Ivy was squeezing my hand so tightly I thought it might burst.

We ran around the front of the building to the side of the school and on to the grass below the window. A swarm of girls was already buzzing around.

"Out of the way!" cried Nurse Gladys.

And I heard, to my relief, a loud moan. As the other girls parted, we saw Josephine lying there. Her eyes were shut, but she was breathing, and her mouth was open.

Not dead. Not dead at all.

I let go of Ivy's hand, which I realized I'd been squeezing just as hard in return.

The matron held up her flashlight, flooding the scene with harsh light. Josephine's skin was scratched and she was covered in leaves and twigs. She must have fallen on to the bush below the window, and it had broken her fall.

Her leg though... It was sticking out at a strange angle. Not right at all.

"She's broken her leg," Clara said, tears streaming down her face. Clara was Josephine's roommate, and she clearly loved her friend, although I'd always thought they were both as poisonous as each other.

"Stand back, please," ordered Nurse Gladys. She crouched down beside the girl in the damp grass, putting her hands either side of her head. It was so wet I could feel the dew seeping through my ruined stockings. "Can you hear me, Josephine?"

"Mmm," Josephine moaned in reply.

"Can you move your leg?"

Josephine shook her head, her lips tight and drawn. "H-hurts...".

"Can you tell me what happened?" the nurse asked, her voice surprisingly calm.

"Can't you see what's happened?" Clara wailed, clutching at her nightgown. "She's fallen out of the window! Oh, it's so awful!"

"Shut up, Clara," said Penny. "We know." For once, I agreed with Penny.

Nurse Gladys glared at them both. "Quiet, please! This is important!" She turned her attention back to Josephine. "Can you tell me what happened?" she repeated.

Josephine mumbled something softly, so softly that none of us could hear.

"Speak up, if you can, dear," the nurse said gently. "How did you fall?"

"I-I..." Josephine started. Her hair blew about her face in the wind. "I didn't fall. I was *pushed*..."

Chapter Seventeen

IVY

As Josephine was taken to the infirmary, we gathered in the foyer, shivering in the night air. Whispers began to spread, and soon the whispers grew into cries.

"Who could have pushed her?"

"Who would do something like that?"

Penny decided to take charge, which was never a good thing. "Listen to me. It can't have been any of us, *obviously*. We all came out of our rooms *after* we heard her scream. So, who's not here?"

Everyone looked at each other suspiciously. There wasn't much light, and it gave all the staring faces a strange, shadowy quality.

All the girls from along our corridor were there. Except...

"Violet!" Ethel shrieked.

I wasn't sure if I was imagining it, but Penny seemed to turn a little green. She'd only just made friends with Violet again—she wanted a witch hunt, but not enough to go after Violet.

"And her crazy friend!" Clara added, tears still staining her cheeks. "What if it was her? My sister said she frightened all the horses away!"

Scarlet stepped forward, furious. "Rose didn't do anything of the sort! How many times do I have to say it? Have you all got cotton wool in your ears?"

The other girls went quiet, turning their stares on my twin.

"It wasn't her," Scarlet said, her fists shaking. "It was—"

She stopped, as if her sentence had run into a brick wall.

I took her hand. Did she believe my theory about Miss Fox, finally? Or did she still suspect Madame Zelda? I wanted to say something, but it sounded like nonsense. Why would Miss Fox risk coming back? Why would she rattle doorknobs and turn loose horses and push girls out of windows? Until I had proof, suggesting it would make me seem like the crazy one.

I felt everyone's eyes on us. "...someone else," I finished for my twin lamely.

I turned to my twin, hoping I'd done the right thing. But her eyes were wide with horror.

Everyone started arguing again, some blaming Rose

and others Violet. I heard Penny shouting something about interrogations. And amid the din, Scarlet dragged me away.

She pulled me over to one corner of the room, next to the door that led to the corridor.

"What is it?" I asked.

Scarlet looked me dead in the eyes. "The blackboard. The horses. And now this? Things are getting worse!"

"Scarlet...it has to be her. Who else would do something like this?" I glanced around fearfully. If Miss Fox had done this... *Was she still here? Was she watching us right now?*

My twin didn't react for a moment. "We can't jump to conclusions," she said, but I had trouble believing that she meant it. I pictured Miss Fox glaring down at us from the balcony that surrounded the double-height foyer. I pictured her stepping through the doorway, cane *swooshing* ahead of her. I pictured her face instead of the faces of the other girls, their eyes filled with anger. Was I going mad?

The door behind us swung open.

I threw myself against the front desk, shaking. Scarlet was beside me, a protective arm cast across my shoulders.

A shape moved through the doorway and resolved itself into the form of the matron.

I should have breathed a sigh of relief then, but I didn't. The danger could be anywhere.

"Girls!" the matron called, looking from us to the big

group that had gathered. "I know you're all in shock, but you *must* return to your beds. Is that clear?"

Penny pushed through the crowd. "But, Miss, we think it might have been—"

The matron frowned. "Penelope Winchester, this is no time for theories. It is time for *bed*. Do you under-stand me? Josephine is being cared for. We will deal with this in the morning."

"But that girl," Penny started, glancing around at everyone else to see if they were behind her. Everyone except Nadia had shrunk back. "Rose, she..."

"In the morning!" the matron snapped. She stood there, eyes narrowed, hair half falling out of its rollers, finger pointed at the door.

I didn't want to argue. The sooner we were back in room thirteen, the sooner we could be wedged in behind the safety of that heavy desk. Even then, I didn't think Scarlet and I would get much sleep that night.

I woke with the morning bell clamoring in my ears and sat bolt upright.

I turned my gaze quickly to Scarlet. She seemed to have built some sort of pillow fort around her head.

I sighed with relief, and it turned into a yawn halfway through. Just as I'd thought, I'd barely slept. I'd kept imagining the events of the night before, over and over. I hadn't seen Josephine fall, but I could play the scene in my head—like going to the pictures.

Josephine messing around by the wide-open window, perhaps leaning out of it, combing her hair.

The dark shadow appearing behind her.

A fierce shove. Josephine losing her balance. Tumbling forward into the night...

It was horrible. I didn't want to think about it, but my mind wouldn't stop. And my fear grew and grew.

"What are we going to do?" I asked Scarlet as we pulled our uniforms on.

Uncharacteristically, she didn't offer any solutions. "Whoever's behind this, we'll stop them," was all she said. But how can you stop someone you can't see? When you don't even know if they're really there?

When we'd moved the desk and escaped our room, I hurried ahead to find Ariadne. She was in the corridor on the way to breakfast, lugging a satchel full of books. "Oh, Ivy!" she said cheerfully. "Good morning! I got up early and went to the library. Miss Jones says she hasn't found that old school photograph for you yet, but she's hoping to get it soon, if you wanted to know."

That was a little disappointing, but it could wait. "Haven't you heard?"

My friend blinked at me. "Heard what?"

I lowered my voice as a troupe of younger girls walked past. "Josephine was pushed out of a window last night!"

Ariadne's hands flew to her mouth. "Oh no! Is she all right? Oh goodness..."

"She's alive," I said quickly. "But I think she broke her leg."

"Wait," said Ariadne, her hands flapping by her sides like a bird. "Pushed? You said 'pushed'! Who pushed her?"

"We don't know. But...do you think it could have been Miss Fox?" I asked, keeping my voice low.

My friend's face went even paler than usual. "I don't know," she whispered. "I'm afraid you could be right."

I swallowed. That wasn't what I wanted to hear. I wanted her to tell me I was being ridiculous. I wanted anything but for it to be true.

We walked into breakfast—and right into a fight.

A gang had crowded around Violet. Clara Brand was at the front, and she'd taken hold of Violet's collar. "Where's the girl?" she was demanding. "Where is she?"

Violet looked furious. "I don't *know*!" she yelled back. "Leave her alone!"

I noticed Penny was there too, hanging behind, looking sheepish.

Ethel was leaning right into Violet's face. "She'd better stop hiding, the little *freak*."

"She must be guilty," said Clara, yanking Violet's

collar harder in her fist. "That's why she's hiding. She pushed Josie, I know it!"

I looked around desperately. Mrs. Knight was nowhere to be seen. My eyes darted to the dinner ladies at the kitchen hatch—even from the other side of the hall, they surely must be able to tell what was going on. But if they could, they seemed to be doing their best to pretend it wasn't happening.

Violet was shaking. If I knew anything about Violet, this wasn't going to end well. "Shut up," she said. "All of you shut up. She's staying out of sight because idiots like *you* keep picking on her. And let go of me, right now." The look she gave Clara was lethal.

"I say we go and find her," said Ethel.

Clara nodded. "And I say we give her a taste of what she did to Josie."

And, just as I took a step forward, Violet picked up her breakfast tray and smacked Clara right in the face. And all hell broke loose.

Chapter Eighteen

SCARLET

The hall was in total chaos.

People were screaming. The sound of smashing china filled the air, not to mention the clatter of utensils being thrown, yells and cries, and the dinner ladies furiously ordering everyone to calm down.

I spotted Ivy and Ariadne hiding under the Evergreen table and ran over to them. Ariadne was wearing an empty porridge bowl like a helmet.

I ducked down in between them. Feet scrambled past us, sliding on spilled breakfast.

"What in the name of *I-don't-even-know-what* is happening?" I shouted, struggling to be heard over the din.

"Fight!" Ariadne shouted back.

"I can see that! Who started it?" I asked.

"Clara!" Ivy yelled. "She thinks Rose pushed

Josephine! She went for Violet and Violet attacked her with a tray!"

I laughed, and Ivy whacked me.

"What? That's funny!" I insisted.

"It's not going to be funny when the teachers get here!" my twin shouted.

It still would be, but I saw her point.

We waited. I watched as some girls scrambled to leave the hall, while others wrestled and kicked each other and threw food. I had to admit, I slightly wanted to join in. But Ivy would have killed me.

"I hope they get here soon!" Ariadne wailed.

It wasn't long before we heard the booming voice of Miss Bowler: *"Everyone freeze! Right now!"*

We watched as the jumbled feet slowly slid to a halt, and the cries died down into stunned silence. There was a final *clang* as a metal tray hit the floor.

"Who started this?"

The silence continued.

"If you don't tell me who started this right this second," Miss Bowler roared, *"every single one of you will have a detention!"*

With that, there was a great shuffling of feet. Ivy, Ariadne, and I slowly peered out from under the table. The crowds of girls had parted like the Red Sea, leaving Violet, Clara, and Ethel in the middle of the room.

Clara was sprawled on the floor, a large red bump forming on her forehead. Violet had Ethel by the throat, her hair was a mess, and both their dresses were ripped.

I clamped a hand over my mouth, trying desperately not to laugh.

"*Right. You* three*! Out!*"

Everyone watched them leave the room. They all looked like they were about to murder each other at the slightest provocation.

"*Everyone else—assembly! Five minutes!*"

❧

It was the most sheepish filing into assembly I'd ever seen. Everyone kept their heads down as if their faces were about to be screamed into at any second. Which was quite likely, really.

"At least," I whispered to Ivy, "they didn't do this when Miss Fox was in charge. Or Mr. Bartholomew."

She nodded. "It would've been canings all around. Or worse."

Ugh. "Worse" was probably right.

We took a seat on one of the benches, and I noticed that Madame Zelda was standing against the wall in the spot usually reserved for Miss Finch. I nudged Ivy and Ariadne, pointing her out.

She was staring at her perfectly manicured nails, looking incredibly bored. She stifled a yawn. *Tired?* I thought. *Up late pushing students out of windows?*

As I thought this, Madame Zelda's gaze flicked up

to me. She stared right into my face as if my suspicions were written all over it. I blinked quickly, and looked away.

I heard Mrs. Knight's heavy steps, as she climbed up to the stage, before I saw her face.

She stood at the lectern, a pile of notes in front of her. "Girls."

She didn't even say "Good morning," and we didn't chorus it back.

"I am *incredibly* disappointed," she began.

Lots of girls were hanging their heads. I fought the urge not to smirk. For once, I hadn't been involved.

"There was a nasty accident in the night." There was a muttering—clearly not everyone had heard the news yet. "One of our students fell from a window and was seriously hurt."

That got some gasps.

"She is currently in the infirmary and is being treated for a broken leg. I'm pleased to report that she seems to be doing well. There has been another incident which is currently being investigated, although we have not been able to find a culprit. And now..." Mrs. Knight peered at us indignantly over her glasses. "I've been informed by Miss Bowler that there has been a *fight* in the breakfast hall. Honestly? Is that any way for young ladies to behave?"

Everyone stayed quiet.

"Rest assured that the instigators will be dealt with," she said, and then sighed loudly, shaking her head.

"And all the rest of you will be going back as soon as this assembly is over to clean up, do you hear me?"

There was a collective moan. Mrs. Knight cut it off quickly, slamming her fist down on the lectern. "Think yourselves lucky! If anything of the sort *ever* happens again, I will be removing privileges from every student. Is that clear?"

"Yes, Miss!" we chorused.

"We have the reputation of the school to think of. And that affects all of us..."

She soared off into a lecture about the proper comportment for a lady, at which point I tuned out.

Once again, I found myself looking at Madame Zelda. She was wearing high heels. I blinked. Could that have been what I'd heard in the corridor last night?

Before I could think any more about it, she was walking forward, and I realized she was taking the stage.

Madame Zelda cleared her throat. "I am here to relay a message from the...*wonderful* Miss Finch."

Her compliment sounded completely false. I glared at her.

"It is about the ballet recital. It is to go ahead as planned, and I am to choose the parts." *Sleeping Beauty* was going ahead, without Miss Finch? With everything else that had been going on, my performance jitters had slipped my mind. Would I be good enough to outshine Penny?

I hated to admit it, but I'd secretly hoped Miss Finch would pick me, because, well—we'd been through a lot together. And perhaps she felt a tiny bit guilty about what her mother had done to me. I shouldn't think that way, but I did.

Madame Zelda though... What chance did I have of getting the role if she was in charge of choosing?

"We will only accept the best," Madame Zelda continued sternly, with no sign of a smile. "So, ensure you get *lots* of practice."

I could have sworn she looked straight at me when she said that. I grabbed a handful of Ivy's dress and tugged it, but she didn't seem to be paying attention. Her face was painted with worry, and she was staring at the ceiling.

Madame Zelda nodded at Mrs. Knight, and then left the stage, her heels clicking on the steps. I clenched my fists. If the odd new teacher was up to something, I was going to find out what.

There was one good thing about having to clean up the mess in the dining hall—we missed a great deal of geography. Who needs geography, anyway? As long as you know where you are, why do you need to know where everything else is?

With the majority of the school pitching in, it should have been a quick job. Aunt Phoebe used to always say "many hands make light work"—but she also used to say "too many cooks spoil the broth," and this seemed to be a case of the second one. Everyone was trying to help, and for a while at least, the mess seemed to be getting worse rather than better. Ariadne was polishing a chair that didn't even have any legs, as they'd all been snapped off.

As I wiped down a tabletop, I had a chance to think. How could I find out about Madame Zelda? No one knew her or knew where she had come from. She was a complete mystery. And her behavior in assembly had convinced me that there was something deeply fishy about her.

There was no way around it: we had to talk to her.

Maybe she would incriminate herself, or at least tell us something useful.

All we needed was the right approach.

✖

At lunchtime, I explained my plan in whispers to Ivy and Ariadne. After everyone's cleaning efforts, we were allowed back in the dining hall, but we had to eat our soup in near-silence. Anything louder than a low muttering got you a deadly glare from Mrs. Knight.

We left the hall as quickly as possible.

"Where do you think Madame Zelda is?" Ariadne asked. "She must eat lunch somewhere..."

"You're assuming she eats food, and isn't a blood-sucking vampire," I said.

That brought me another deadly glare, this time

from Ivy, but since that was like getting one from a kitten, I wasn't entirely bothered.

"Let's check the ballet studio first," I said.

We went down there, but the office was locked shut. "Perhaps she goes to the staff room?" Ivy suggested.

"I hope not," I said. "Because there's no way I'm going to try sneaking in there."

Ivy rolled her eyes. "We don't have to *sneak in.* There's such a thing as knocking on the door and asking to speak with someone, you know. We can say we need to ask her about the ballet recital."

"I think we *do* need to ask her about the ballet recital," I said carefully. "Come on."

Without explaining myself, I led them off toward the staff room. It was a place I usually avoided. The words "Staff Only" were painted in big black letters on a wooden sign over the door.

I took a deep breath and raised my fist to knock, only for the door to swing open and bring me face to face with Madame Zelda.

Chapter Nineteen

IVY

Madame Zelda looked down at us as if we were unexpected rocks in her path.

"Yes?" she said, with that hint of an unusual accent at the edge of her voice. "Did you want something?"

"W-we wanted to speak with you, Miss," I said, not sure why I was suddenly nervous. Perhaps Scarlet's suspicions were having an effect. "About the ballet recital."

"Ah!" She nodded, a quick jerk of the head. "Come with me. Now!"

She darted away down the corridor, her walking almost as graceful as her dancing—even in impossibly high heels. How did she do that?

I glanced quickly at Ariadne, who made a noise a bit like *welp*. "Perhaps I'll just go to the library and meet you later?" she said, as if it were a suggestion, but she was already leaving halfway through the sentence.

Reluctantly, I followed Scarlet and Madame Zelda.

She led us outside, where the day was brightening. It was fairly warm and lots of girls had headed out after finishing their lunch. The cawing of the rooks was in the air, as were cries of first years running around, and the general sound of chatter as everyone gossiped—most likely about Josephine and the Grand Battle of Breakfast.

We stood and watched as Madame Zelda pulled out an incense stick and lit it with a match from her pocket. She held it out in front of her like a sword, a waft of pale-blue smoke trailing from the stick up into the air. The strong smell of spice hit my nose. "Merely a personal ritual," she said, seeing our baffled expressions. "It clears the air, and the mind." She inhaled deeply through her nose, as if to make a point. "Now. You wished to speak with me about the recital?"

"Um, yes, Miss," Scarlet said. "It's about what you said in assembly. I was worried that the recital wouldn't go ahead."

Madame Zelda raised her eyebrows. "Of course! It's an important part of the school calendar. Why ever wouldn't it?"

"Well, we thought, with Miss Finch away—" I started.

"Pah." She waved the incense stick near my face, making me cough. "We do not need Rebecca Finch."

The way she said it gave me pause. "You...know her, Miss?"

"Pah," she said again. "Ancient history." But she

had that look on her face that people sometimes have when they secretly want to tell you more, like the words are just waiting to be drawn from their lips.

"When you were younger...?" I asked, not quite believing my own ears.

"We were at the Academy of Dance together," Madame Zelda said, with a sharpness in her voice. "Rebecca was the *favorite*. Everyone felt sorry for her, so they gave her everything. Poor little orphan Rebecca. She wasn't even a real orphan. She was adopted." She gripped the incense stick in both hands, as if she were about to snap it in two. "I was the better dancer, and no one could see it."

"So, this was before her accident?" Scarlet asked. Miss Finch had fallen from the stage one night while performing—that was how her leg had been crippled.

Madame Zelda blinked down at my twin. "How did you know about that?"

"She told us," Scarlet shrugged.

"Well," Madame Zelda said, suddenly staring at nothing. "Was that all you wanted to ask?"

I looked at my twin, wondering if she was going to start her interrogation. But instead she just said, "I wanted to know who you think will get the roles." She was tangling her fingers together.

"It is my duty to choose the best dancers," the new teacher answered, her chest swelling with pride. "It will be a most difficult and important task."

I tried to keep the frown from my face. Madame Zelda seemed all too eager to replace Miss Finch.

Deciding to change the subject, I blurted out, "Do you know anything about what happened to the horses, Miss? Or Josephine?"

She blinked at me this time, and when she finally spoke, all she said was, "I'm not a fan of horses. Too hairy. And I do not know this Josephine. Now, I must be going." She snuffed out the incense stick and slid it back into a slim pocket. "Off to your lessons, girls."

"Yes, Miss," I said dutifully.

When we were at a safe distance away, I glanced back, only to see that Madame Zelda had disappeared.

"Well that was extremely odd," I said to Scarlet.

But Scarlet was off in her own world. "Only the best," she whispered, her eyes wide.

I snapped my fingers in front of her as we walked. "Scarlet! There will be time for worrying about ballet later! You saw how strange she was acting. And didn't you hear what she said? You might have been right all along!"

My twin turned to me. "Only the best will be chosen..." she droned.

"Wake up!" I gave her a gentle prod in the arm. "She knew Miss Finch in school and they were *rivals*."

"So?" said Scarlet.

"So," I replied. "Isn't that *motive*?"

❧

When we got to French, Ariadne was already seated.

I slid into the desk next to her and was just about to tell her what we'd learned when Madame Boulanger walked in.

"*Bonjour la classe!*" she said cheerfully.

I shot Ariadne an apologetic look. As Madame Boulanger began writing verbs on the blackboard, I tore a piece of lined paper from my notebook as quietly as possible. As I did so, it occurred to me that passing notes wasn't a very Ivy thing to do. All that time pretending to be Scarlet had clearly rubbed off on me.

A—

MZ acting strangely. Turns out she knew MFi in the past! They were rivals!

—I

I folded the paper a few times and then flicked the little bundle on to Ariadne's desk.

I watched out of the corner of my eye as she read it and then quickly scrambled for her ink pen.

I smirked a little. Ariadne wasn't very good at subtlety.

A short time later, she passed the note back to me.

Gosh, that is truly suspicious. Perhaps we should try and find out more about her.

Love from Ariadne. xxx

I rolled my eyes and picked up my pen again.

A—

you're not supposed to put your name
and kisses on a secret note.

                                        —I

I handed it back, and a few moments later came
the reply:

Oh, I'm such a fool! Sorry, Ivy!

I started sniggering. Scarlet noticed and gave me
a funny look. Thank goodness Madame Boulanger
was incredibly unobservant when she was engrossed
in conjugations.

☙

We all retreated to room thirteen after the bell rang for
the end of class.

"So, do you think Madame Zelda is behind all of it?
Miss Finch and the horses and the creepy message
and Josephine?" Ariadne asked, perching on the edge
of my bed.

"*Yes*," said Scarlet.

I paused before answering. "I really don't know. She
had reason to get rid of Miss Finch, that's for sure. But
the other things? What could she be trying to achieve?"

"Maybe she wants to scare us," said Ariadne, but
she seemed unconvinced.

"If only we could actually *prove* it." Scarlet sighed. "Then everyone would leave Rose alone. She's been in hiding because of all this."

I raised an eyebrow. Scarlet seemed to be getting more attached to Rose. When we'd had to look after her last term, Scarlet had been less than pleased, but now she truly cared about the poor abandoned girl, and I wondered where her change of heart had come from.

"We ought to search Madame Zelda's office for evidence," Ariadne said, pointing into the air dramatically. "We'll find something that gives her away, and when she least expects it..." she slammed her fist down on to the bed, making me jump.

"I hate to break it to you," Scarlet said, "but the office in the studio is usually empty. I don't know if she even uses it."

"Oh," Ariadne said, looking completely crushed.

"We'll just have to watch her." My twin started pacing up and down. "We'll see if she says anything that might give us a clue as to what she's up to."

I closed my eyes and lay back against the cold pillow. Once again, it seemed we had no hope. Miss Fox, or Madame Zelda, or whoever it was, was closing in. And now someone had been badly hurt.

Who would be next?

Chapter Twenty

SCARLET

I wasn't sure whether I wanted to impress Madame Zelda or have her locked up. It all depended on whether or not she really was guilty.

Without any real proof, I had to assume she wasn't (though that annoyed me a lot). And that meant the recital was still on, and I *had* to be the best. But with no Miss Finch to give me extra practice, how was that going to happen?

That night, I decided to take matters into my own hands and practice.

Of course, I didn't leave room thirteen. There was no chance of me doing that with an evil window-pusher lurking around the corner. I wasn't crazy.

Instead, I waited for Ivy to go to sleep, and then I peeled back the sheets from my bed and pulled on my toe shoes. There wasn't much space to practice, but I could do stretches and try to perfect my positions.

I kept an ear out for anyone in the corridor, just in case. There was nothing—until a sudden *bang* came from outside, and I tripped over the leg of the bed and went sprawling on to the floor. For a few moments, I just lay there on the carpet, frozen in panic.

I tried to slow my breathing. It was probably someone slamming a door or a window moving in the wind.

I felt so cold and alone, even with Ivy right there next to me. We were so lost. Everything was going wrong. There was nothing we could do to keep everyone safe or prove Madame Zelda was involved or stop everyone bullying Rose or... The list went on and on.

Dancing in the dark was more trouble than it was worth. I climbed back into bed with my head spinning and all these fears tumbling through my mind.

I was standing in a room, one that was more than familiar. I looked around. Twin beds. A tall mirror between them. It was our bedroom, back home.

I looked at myself in the mirror and saw the reflection. I couldn't quite keep my eyes on it—it kept flickering and changing. One minute it looked more like me. The next, it looked more like Ivy.

And then, as I stood there, something appeared behind me. The shadow.

I wanted to run. But my feet were rooted to the spot.

The shadow came closer and reached out a hand. It placed it on my shoulder.

Something stirred inside me. A memory. I'd felt that touch before, a long time ago.

Slowly, I willed myself to turn. "Mother?" I asked.

But when I looked around, the shadow had melted away into nothing.

∞

When I woke up the next morning, things seemed a little clearer. How does that happen? It's like your brain sorts through everything while you're asleep, and sometimes it comes up with the right answer. Or, at least, an answer that stops you feeling like everything is impossible.

My strange dream had somehow been comforting. We had to carry on searching for our mother. Maybe we'd find nothing. Maybe we'd find out she hated us, and we'd be more alone than ever. But at least we'd know *something*.

That was why I dragged Ivy to the library while she was still yawning sleepily and had only half-brushed her hair.

We found Miss Jones at the front desk, looking unusually excited.

"Oh, girls!" she said as soon as we walked in. "I have something for you."

I grinned at Ivy. "See," I said. "I knew it!"

"Muh," was all she replied, halfway through a yawn.

Miss Jones put her bag on the desk and began rifling through it. "I had to go home, you see." She paused. "It was lovely to see Mama again. She makes the most wonderful rice dishes. Of course, it means I have to see Symphony." She made a face.

"You have to see a symphony?" Ivy asked sleepily.

"What? Oh, no. She's my sister, you see," Miss Jones explained. "I was always jealous that she got the prettiest name. No one likes a catastrophe, do they? But everyone enjoys a symphony..." She sighed. "Ah!"

She pulled out a paper folder, and when she opened it up we saw a photographic print inside. Unmistakably a school photograph, with rows and rows of students.

I gasped and leaned forward as she spun the photograph around to face us.

Miss Jones picked up a pencil from her neatly arranged stash and pointed to one of the girls in the near front row. "I stared at this picture for a long time, trying to search my memory. And I *think* this right here was Emmeline Adel, the girl who...drowned in the lake. And this next to her—" she moved the pencil over one.

I saw it immediately.

Emmeline could not have been our mother. She looked so different; a long, thin face and pale blond hair. But the girl next to her, on the other hand...

"She looks just like us," I said, in awe.

Ivy nodded, her mouth silently hanging open.

It was a little hard to make out—the photograph was old and the faces small, but there was the same dark hair, the same porcelain features.

And what gave it away even more than that was the necklace. "Look," I said, tapping the photograph with my finger.

You weren't supposed to wear jewelry at Rookwood, but I could see a little string of pearls. The very same string that Ivy had inherited.

"That's her!" I cried. "That's our mother!" A fellow rule-breaker too. I felt a hint of pride.

Miss Jones grinned, evidently pleased as punch. "She and Emmeline were best friends, I think."

"Wait," said Ivy.

I stopped, suddenly wary. "What?"

"Look up there." This time it was Ivy's turn to point at the photograph. It took me a moment, but I soon saw what she meant.

A few rows behind, where the girls looked a little taller and older, there was *another* face that looked just like ours. And as my eye slipped downward, I realized that she *too* was wearing a pearl necklace.

Now it was my turn for my mouth to drop open. "*Sisters?*"

❧

Miss Jones took the photograph over to one side of the library, where there were high desks with green-shaded reading lamps over them. Ivy and I looked at each other in complete shock.

"I wrote everyone's initials on the back," the librarian explained. "There wasn't room for full names, unfortunately. But perhaps this will jog my memory." She flattened out the picture on the desk and switched on the lamp, pouring a warm glow over rows and rows of initials.

We leaned over and watched as she ran her finger along the letters on the lower row, until she reached *EA*. She paused, and then moved to the inscription just to the right. *IJS*.

Ivy and I looked up at her expectantly.

"IJS, IJS..." Miss Jones patted her finger against her lip. "Oh! Yes! I think that girl's name was *Ida*. Does that sound right?"

I shrugged. I had no idea. It could be. *Ida*. Was that our mother's true name?

"Is there any way you can check the name?" Ivy asked. "Find her surname, and her...sister's?"

"Certainly," Miss Jones replied as the school bell began to ring. "I can look for the initials in the school attendance records for that year. Come back at lunchtime, and I'll have an answer for you."

❧

The morning dragged. I was desperate to know who our mother was, who her *sister was*. Lunchtime took forever to arrive.

First, in assembly, Mrs. Knight gave us an update on Josephine. She'd been taken to the nearest hospital to have her leg put in a cast, apparently. Clara tearfully asked if she would be coming back. Mrs. Knight shook her head and told us that Josephine's parents wanted her to stay home and rest.

"Meaning they don't want her at school with a murderer on the loose," I whispered to Ivy.

"Scarlet!" Ivy whispered back. "It's not technically a murderer if nobody died."

"Close enough," I said.

Lunch finally came, and we returned to the library, this time with Ariadne in tow. Ivy had filled her in about what Miss Jones had found that morning. I was practically buzzing.

The librarian was in the middle of teaching Anna Santos the Dewey decimal system.

"So you see, nine hundred is for history and geography..." she was saying.

I cleared my throat.

"Oh, hello again, girls," she smiled, full of pride. Then she paused and handed Anna a stack of books with numbers written on the spines. "Here," she told her assistant, "you can practice putting these in the right categories."

When Anna had waddled off uncertainly into the stacks, Miss Jones turned back to us.

"You found their mother, Miss?" Ariadne asked, wide-eyed with excitement.

"Well, I think so." Miss Jones nodded. She pulled out a heavy brown folder that looked a good twenty years old, and heaved it open to a page she'd marked. "Luckily there was only one person with the initials IJS in that year."

We waited, those few seconds seeming like hours, as Miss Jones ran her pencil down the list.

"Ida Jane Smith. That was her name."

I let out a gasp. It was so strange to hear it said aloud. As if it made her *real*, somehow. And it sounded almost familiar, but I couldn't place why. Was it something I'd heard long ago?

"And the sister?" Ivy asked.

"I checked the initials on the back of the photo— hers were SLS." Miss Jones turned a few pages in the folder. "This one was a little trickier, but once I figured out which form she was in I tracked her down. Sara Louise Smith."

Ariadne was grinning at us madly. "You realize what this means?"

I looked at her blankly. "What?"

"You have an aunt," she said. "An aunt who *might still be alive!*"

Chapter Twenty-One

IVY

Knowing that we had an aunt changed everything.

Of course, it wasn't as if she was our only one. We had sweet, scatterbrained Aunt Phoebe on our father's side, who I cared for dearly.

But this was different. Sara had known our mother when she was young. She'd known *Ida*, not *Emmeline*! If she was alive, what could she tell us about her?

There was just one problem: we had absolutely no idea where to find our new aunt.

Hope dangled tantalizingly out of reach.

My mind raced. This list of things I'd known about our mother had gone from:

1. Her maiden name was Emmeline Adel.
2. She'd been born on January the first, 1899.

3. She'd once owned a monogrammed silver hairbrush and a string of pearls.

To the longer and more puzzling:

1. Her maiden name was Ida Jane Smith.
2. She had been a student at Rookwood School.
3. She'd been best friends with a girl named Emmeline Adel, who drowned after being forced to swim in the lake by Headmaster Bartholomew.
4. She'd taken on Emmeline's identity (reason unknown).
5. She had an older sister named Sara Louise Smith.
6. She once owned a monogrammed silver hairbrush as well as a string of pearls <u>that matched her sister's.</u>

I wrote that list down on a piece of scrap paper that evening in our room and stared at it. It had always seemed strange to know so little about the person who'd brought us into the world. Now we knew more, but in some ways...less. There were so many questions and not an answer to be found.

I opened up the desk drawer and looked at the string of pearls curled around the hairbrush. The engraving on the back, **EG**...that was wrong, I thought. She should've been Ida Jane Gray, **IJG**, not Emmeline Gray. Why had she taken her dead friend's identity?

And the pearls: her sister had owned some just the same. Was that why the necklace had been important to her? It had always seemed an unusual heirloom, and to leave that and nothing else...

I spun around on the chair and looked at Scarlet, who was being strangely quiet. She was lying on her bed, staring at the ceiling. "What are you thinking about?" I asked.

"Everything," she responded. "Well, I keep trying to think about our mother, but I get stuck, because I don't know enough to think about her properly. And then I remember the ballet recital, and I just..." she trailed off.

I gulped. I kept trying to forget about the ballet recital. Of course, I loved ballet. It had always been my favorite thing to do. But performing on a stage, in front of everyone... The thought made me feel a little sick.

Scarlet was scared that she might not get the lead role. I was scared of having to take part at all. I hoped to be given the tiniest part somewhere in the back, so that no one would notice if I made a complete fool of myself.

"You'll get the part," I reassured her.

She perked up at that. "Do you really think so?"

"Of course," I said. "You work so hard at ballet." And not at much else, I didn't add.

"But," she said, picking at loose threads on her sheets. "Do I want to be chosen by Madame Zelda? What if she's really evil?"

I gave my twin a look. "Maybe she's up to something. Or hiding something. But I don't think she's *evil*."

Scarlet sighed.

Friday came, which at least meant we would have a chance to keep an eye on Madame Zelda at the ballet lesson that afternoon.

But before that...there was something else.

Before that, the letters started.

Friday assembly meant letters. It was when the teachers handed out the mail that had been received for students during the week.

It was always met with excitement, whether people were getting letters or packages from friends or family. I always hoped to get something from Aunt Phoebe, even though she was usually just asking things like where she might have left the can opener. We would all gather around to read and discuss whatever had been sent.

What nobody expected, though, was for Penny to receive a letter that caused her to burst out crying, throw it on to the floor, and run out of the hall.

"What on earth..." I began, but Scarlet was quicker than me. While everyone was staring, she had shot over to where Penny had been standing and picked up the piece of paper.

In seconds, there was a crowd of girls around her peering over her shoulder.

"Nosey," she said, clutching it to her chest.

"Oh, come on, Scarlet," said Nadia and tried to grab it off her. "We need to know what it says!"

Scarlet waved it at her. "Fine then, let's see."

I pushed through the group and watched as Scarlet unfolded the page. It was written on a typewriter, and it read:

> Dear Penny,
>   You're such a show-off. You think you're a perfect prefect. You think you're so wonderful at ballet. You won't ever be the best, not at anything. You're nothing but a fake, a pretender, second best.
>   No one loves you, can't you see that? Not even your precious mummy and daddy. Not even your friends.

There was no signature. Ethel picked up the discarded envelope and examined it, but there was nothing to give away the sender there either: the address label was typewritten, and it hadn't been sealed.

Nadia looked suspiciously at Scarlet. "Did you write this?"

"Me?" Scarlet said. "Why would I?"

"Because you hate her," Nadia rightly pointed out.

Scarlet made a face. "I dashed over to read it, didn't I? Why would I do that if I'd written it?"

"Yes," said Nadia flatly, "but then you tried to not show it to us. Maybe you were hiding the evidence?"

"Oh, for goodness' sake," my twin snapped. "I have better things to do with my time than concoct elaborate schemes to insult Penny. I'll just insult her to her face, thank you very much." She shoved the letter into Nadia's hands and stalked out.

I stood in a flurry of gossip as everyone gave their opinions on who'd sent the letter. Some people seemed to believe it was Scarlet, but there were plenty of other suggestions. Penny had a lot of enemies.

"Maybe it was from Violet," someone whispered in my ear.

I jumped, only to find Ariadne beside me.

"Sorry!" she said. "Don't you think it could have been?"

I shook my head. "It might have been Violet's style in the past, but now..." We looked over at Violet, but she didn't even seem to have noticed the commotion. She was sitting in a corner with Rose, chatting away about something.

I began trying to push my way out of the jabbering crowd, hoping to head after Scarlet.

"But Penny accused Rose, didn't she?" Ariadne said, walking along next to me, and that made me think a little harder. "And they're so close."

"Well, I'm sure Violet's angry about that. But I'm not sure if it's enough to do this," I replied.

"Do you think we should...find Penny?" she asked. "See if she's all right?"

I stopped. "Really?"

"Well, she seemed quite upset. It was rather nasty, wasn't it?"

Ariadne amazed me sometimes. If that girl could care about someone as mean as Penny, there was nothing she couldn't do.

❧

Penny was in the lavatories. She wasn't too difficult to find, given the sound of loud sniffing that was coming from one of the stalls.

Ariadne knocked gently on the door. "Penny?"

"Go away!" came the reply, followed by a succession of angry sniffs.

"We just came to see if you were all right," Ariadne explained.

There were a few moments of quiet, and then Penny flung open the door. Her freckled cheeks were dripping with tears, and her eyes were red and puffy. "If your sister put you up to this, I'm going to kill her!"

"I don't even know where Scarlet is," I protested. "And she didn't write that letter, honestly."

Penny shot me a deadly glare and slid down on to the floor as if her legs had forgotten how to work.

Ariadne patted her on the shoulder. "There, there," she said. If anyone else had done that it would have been incredibly patronizing, but Ariadne meant it sincerely.

"Why would anyone *hate* me?" Penny moaned.

I tried to hold my tongue. I could give her a pretty long list of reasons. But I didn't want to aggravate her any further. Not to mention the fact that I didn't want to stoop to her level (and I meant that literally as well; I didn't fancy sitting on the lavatory floor).

She looked up at us, brushing the angry tears away from her face. "Stay away from me, do you hear?" she snapped. "And if I find out Scarlet did this..." She clenched her shaking fists.

"All right, all right, we'll leave you alone," I said. I ushered Ariadne back outside. There really was no helping Penny.

※

I expected that to be the end of it. I didn't have a clue who'd sent that mean letter. And, well, this was *Penny*. She'd dished out so much nastiness over the years that it wasn't surprising people wanted to give a little back. It was probably a one-time thing.

Or so I thought, until we got to Latin class.

Miss Simons was sitting at her desk in silence, staring out of the window. She was wringing her hands and looked clearly distressed.

Scarlet had got there already, since she'd left

assembly before anyone else. But she was just sitting at her desk, doing nothing. I looked at her and she raised her hands into the air. "I'm not touching this one," was all she said.

"What's the matter, Miss?" Ariadne asked.

Miss Simons turned her head. Her neatly applied makeup was all smudged. "Oh, it's awful," she said in a small voice. "I simply... I simply cannot teach under these circumstances. Class will have to be canceled today."

She stood up and swept out of the room.

I looked down at the desk and saw the note.

Dear Miss Simons,
    Latin is a dead language. Why do you even bother?
    PS I know what you said about Miss Danver. Whatever will she think when she finds out? You will pay for what you've done.

Chapter Twenty-Two

SCARLET

"*I wonder what* she said about Miss Danver? It must have been pretty awful," I said to Ivy once she showed me the note. Miss Danver was the physics teacher and fairly unassuming. Ivy gave me a despairing look, as if to say that wasn't the point.

But then we heard the commotion coming from the corridor.

Miss Simons hadn't made it far. She'd been cornered by Miss Danver, who was waving a piece of paper in her face.

"Did you say this?" Miss Danver was demanding, her face bright red. "Did you? I want an answer!"

"No, I never said..." Miss Simons was choking through tears. The rest of our Latin class were behind them in the corridor, watching eagerly.

Miss Danver tore the paper into tiny pieces. "I've had enough of your lies, Samantha!"

"Please," Miss Simons begged, "not in front of the girls. I'll be fired..."

"As well you should be!" the physics teacher pointed a quivering finger right into our Latin teacher's face. "I hope I never have to see you again!" She threw the pieces of the offending note into a nearby wastepaper basket and stalked away, fists clenched.

We stared at Miss Simons, unsure what to do. She looked around at all the eyes on her, burst into sobs and ran off down the corridor.

✂

While someone went to fetch Mrs. Knight, we wandered the corridors. That was when we heard a commotion coming from the entrance hall.

A group of girls was anxiously chattering in front of the bulletin board, which seemed to have acquired a new notice.

NOTICE
Rookwood School is no longer safe
Leave before it's too late
And stay away from windows...

I went to grab it, but suddenly the caretaker had stepped in front of me and plucked it from the board.

"I'll take that!" he said. He crumpled it up and shoved it into the pocket of his overalls.

"But, sir," said one of the girls, a first year with her stockings pulled up far too high and a satchel that was bigger than she was, "is it true? Do we have to leave?"

He pointed a finger at her. "Just forget you ever saw this, young lady." He trudged away, angrily muttering something about pranksters and children having no respect these days.

❧

At lunchtime, I called a crisis meeting. It involved Ivy, Ariadne, and I sitting around a tree with sandwiches and wearing serious faces while we discussed who might have sent the letters. The sun was out, but there was still a chill in the air.

"I think it must have been the same person," I said. "The letters and the notice were all typewritten."

"Anyone could use a typewriter though," said Ariadne.

"Well, yes," I conceded. "But what are the chances of three separate people sending nasty notes on the same day?"

"Four," Ivy pointed out. "Miss Danver got one too."

"I thought it might have been a student that sent the one to Penny," Ivy said, her sandwich not yet touched. "But would a student send insults to teachers?" She looked at me. "Present company excluded, of course."

I frowned. "Even I wouldn't go that far! And besides, how would a student know about what Miss Simons supposedly said?" Unless they were eavesdropping, I guessed.

Ariadne was halfway through a bite of her sandwich when she said, "mmmfhh mmmfgh mmmf?"

"What?" Ivy and I said in unison.

She swallowed. "I said, what if it was another teacher? Who sent the letters?"

Someone sprang to mind immediately. Could she be behind this too?

"And more importantly," Ariadne continued, "*why*?"

We had sewing before ballet and I managed to prick myself with the needle about a dozen times. At least the time passed without anyone else getting an insulting letter.

I walked into the studio a bundle of nerves. Madame Zelda was standing at the front of the class, holding her position like a statue. At first I thought there was something wrong, and I squeezed Ivy's hand. Perhaps she *had* had a letter and had gone into shock.

But as the class filed in, she began to speak. "Ballet is about movement. But it is also about control. First, you control your mind. Then, you control your body. Absolute control at all times."

She slowly stretched her leg toward the ceiling,

impossibly high, with barely a wobble, her chin lifted skyward. (Or toward where the sky would have been, were we not underground.)

"You will learn control. The first part of that, the simplest part, is to remain completely silent. For this lesson, there will be no talking from the class. You will focus on my instruction and the music and your own body. Is that understood?"

Several people opened their mouths to say "Yes, Miss," before realizing the smart thing to do was to simply nod.

"Wonderful. Let us begin."

$\mathcal{L}$

I tried my absolute best to stay silent as we danced. Penny was staring daggers at me as she passed, and I could tell it infuriated her that she couldn't shout at me. I just smiled and ignored her. I couldn't risk getting into trouble.

We were learning the dances from *Sleeping Beauty* for our performance—it wouldn't be the full version of the ballet, but a shorter one.

And I tried harder than I've ever tried before. Penny, on the other hand, wasn't on form. She kept quivering, clearly horrified at the prospect of being second best to me. Ha!

Ivy was doing well, but I could tell she was trying her hardest to fade into the background. Typical Ivy.

"Well done, girls," Madame Zelda said as we concluded *reverence*. "You have worked hard today."

This was met with silence.

"Oh." She waved a hand. "And you may speak again."

I grabbed hold of Ivy. "Were you hiding behind me?"

She looked sheepish. "Maybe. It's just... I know you want the main part. And I *don't*. I don't think I want a part at all."

I gaped at her. "Why not?"

She sat down on the floor and began unlacing her shoes. "All those people in the audience... What if I humiliate myself?"

I sat down beside her. "You're my twin. You have to be up there with me. You remember the deal, don't you?"

Ivy paused for a moment and then slowly smiled. "*We'll go to America and we'll be famous, because we're twins.*"

She was quoting me, when we were younger. I'd been convinced we were both destined for fame and fortune. In a way, I still was.

I mean, I'd be *more* famous. But Ivy would be by my side. Or else what was the point?

"We'll get you on that stage. Even if you don't have the most amazing part, you'll still be wonderful." I started unlacing my own shoes, and my twin smiled and leaned her head on my shoulder.

And for a few moments, I forgot the chaos of the school, and I just felt good.

Chapter Twenty-Three

IVY

Scarlet practically danced out of the studio when the lesson was over. I hung back near the stairs, wondering if Madame Zelda would do anything suspicious. But as soon as the girls started leaving, she darted swiftly to the office, and I heard an unfamiliar click as she locked the door. Hmm.

Unfortunately, I was so busy watching Madame Zelda that I didn't notice I was left alone with Penny.

Suddenly, she shoved me against the wall, hard. I felt the rough stone cut into my head. "Ow!"

"Did Scarlet send those letters?" Penny demanded.

"No!" I cried. "Let go, you're hurting me!"

"I don't think I will," she sneered. The pain burned. "Your sister thinks she can mess with me," she muttered. Then she looked up at me again, sharply. "But I can mess with *you*." She pushed me back harder.

"Ow!" I cried again. Couldn't Madame Zelda hear this? I could hear the swift clack of typewriter keys coming from her office. I wriggled and tried to squirm away from Penny.

"Eventually you'll crack," she said with a poisonous glare. "You'll tell her. And you know what'll happen then, don't you?"

Scarlet will be furious and jeopardize her part in the ballet, I thought. Or even worse. I couldn't let that happen. I stayed silent.

Penny dropped me and stepped away. I groaned and felt the back of my head. When I took my finger away, there was a small spot of blood.

"You can show her that," said Penny. "And you can tell her it's from me." She stalked off haughtily, leaving me alone under the flickering gas lights of the studio.

I wanted to cry. But I couldn't say a word. I quickly plaited my hair over the cut so that Scarlet wouldn't see. What else could I do?

Soon it was the weekend, which usually meant that we got a chance to relax and have a little fun. But that weekend, it seemed things were destined to keep going wrong.

We walked to Kendall and Smith's, the grocery shop in Rookwood village. Ariadne had a purse bulging with coins as usual, hoping to buy more midnight feast sweets. Scarlet and I had very little, but thankfully Ariadne was very generous with her sweets.

It was cloudy, and the sun was weak, but at least it wasn't raining. The clouds flowed overhead as if someone were pouring them into the sky.

And right outside the shop, there was a fight going on. Two older girls, who I didn't quite recognize, were screaming at each other while a crowd looked on.

"I never went near him!" yelled one of them, a tall girl with auburn hair.

"I don't believe it!" the other one shouted back. "We all know what you're like! This just *proves* it."

And suddenly they'd leaped at each other, wrestling and pulling each other's hair and aiming blows. I was frozen in place, mentally reliving the fight I'd had with Penny outside this very shop.

Luckily, it wasn't long before their friends began to pull them apart (or at least some of their friends— others were still cheering them on).

Scarlet looked at me. "Another note, you think?"

I nodded. "Looks like it."

Ariadne looked worried. "What if one of us gets one?"

"That would be brilliant!" said Scarlet. We both looked at her. "Because it would be evidence? It might give us a clue."

I wasn't sure it would be especially great, particularly if it caused us to have a huge falling-out. "Come on," I said, trying to keep up a cheerful exterior. "Let's go. Sweets!"

∽

We returned from the shop with two paper bags full of sweets, Ariadne already munching happily. As we walked into the foyer, we saw Mrs. Knight standing at the front desk. She looked as if she were about to tear her hair out.

"Miss?" Scarlet said quizzically as we approached.

"This is a nightmare," I heard Mrs. Knight mutter under her breath. But then she turned to face us. "Oh, hello, girls. Just a little...problem, that's all."

We stared at her.

It was Ariadne who broke the silence. "Are you sure everything's okay, Miss?"

Mrs. Knight sighed deeply. "It's Miss Flit," she said. She gestured toward the empty seat behind the front desk. Usually Rookwood's anxious secretary was sitting there, shuffling things. "She appears to have run away."

Scarlet frowned. "Why?"

"I don't know," the acting headmistress replied. She waved a folded piece of paper at us. "She just left a note on the desk saying that she's sorry and she can't take it anymore. She says she's going to become a florist..."

I had a feeling I knew what might have caused her to take such drastic action. "Did she get a letter, by any chance?"

"I haven't found one," Mrs. Knight said. She looked at me pointedly. "Is there something I should know? Is this to do with what happened between Miss Danver and Miss Simons earlier today?"

"Not just them," Ariadne said. "Some of the girls have got letters as well." She paused and then added in a whisper, "*not very nice ones.*"

Mrs. Knight's brow knitted. "Excuse me, girls. I need to think about this." She took Miss Flit's folded letter and strode away in the direction of her office.

How many more people would be casualties of these letters?

"You know," I said, turning to my friends with a feeling of dread, "I could've sworn I heard Madame Zelda typing in her office after ballet today."

Scarlet clenched her fists. Ariadne just looked puzzled. "Isn't that what you usually do in an office?"

"I *suppose*," said Scarlet begrudgingly. But she didn't look convinced.

❧

We spent the rest of Saturday hidden away in our room. I helped Ariadne with her knitting—not that she really needed help, but I could at least hold the wool—while Scarlet endlessly practiced her ballet. I was really hoping that we would avoid any further drama.

At dinner, Mrs. Knight stood up and demanded that there was to be *no trouble of any kind*, glaring at the

assembled students. Our normally sunny headmistress was clearly getting to the end of her tether.

Some people even started being overly polite in
her presence, as if that would help. Ethel asked
me to "please pass the salt, thank you very much,"
which was probably the nicest thing she'd ever said
to me.

As Ariadne went off to her dorm, armed with more
sweets, Scarlet and I went into the bathrooms to
brush our teeth. When we stepped out, I heard the
sound of crying from farther down the corridor.

Oh no. Not again.

I looked at Scarlet, who immediately rolled her
eyes. "Oh, come on, do we really want to know?"

I wasn't sure if I did. Part of me wanted to just shut
myself back in our room and not deal with it... And if
Scarlet was going to...

No. I was Ivy, not Scarlet. I didn't have to always go
along with her.

"We should take a look," I said firmly. Scarlet looked
annoyed, but this time she didn't disagree.

We walked down to find the door of one of the
rooms ajar and the sound of loud sobbing coming
from within.

I knocked gently on the door and then peered in.
It was Clara, curled up on her bed in a flood of tears.
The opposite bed was empty.

I wasn't even remotely surprised to see a piece of
paper in her hands.

"Oh, Clara," I said, feeling sorry for her even after all she'd done. I walked in and sat down on her bed. "What does it say?"

Without a break in her sobbing, she handed the letter to me.

Dear Clara,
    You are a nasty, nasty girl. Is it
any wonder that you lost your best
friend? It was your fault that she fell
from that window. You should have
saved her.
    Leave the school while you still
can. Everyone will turn on you when
they realize what a bully you are...

As I finished reading, Clara suddenly sat up and grabbed my arm. "I'm so sorry," she wailed. "I didn't mean any of it!"

"Any of what?" said Scarlet. She was leaning in the doorway, her arms folded.

"I've been awful." She gulped and sobbed. "I shouldn't have attacked Violet. I shouldn't have shouted and I shouldn't have picked on everyone..."

"It's all right—" I started.

"No," said Scarlet. "Let her apologize. She should."

I glared at my twin. "Scarlet, she's just received a horrible letter."

Scarlet stepped into the room. "Clara, listen, you

didn't push Josephine from that window, so it wasn't your fault."

Clara sniffed. "Poor Josie. I miss her so much."

"But you are a bully," Scarlet continued, arms still crossed. "And you shouldn't have attacked Violet or blamed Rose. Maybe you should go and apologize to them."

My mouth was hanging open a little. I don't think this was quite the response Clara had been expecting either.

Scarlet turned to me. "These letters are getting to everyone because they're *true*. I mean, not all of it, and they're excessively cruel. But it's the grains of truth that are getting everyone upset."

Clara threw herself back down on to the bed and buried her face in the pillow.

"What are you getting at?" I asked Scarlet.

My twin plucked the letter from my hands. "Whoever wrote these," she said, holding it out in the light, "they're watching us. All of us."

Chapter Twenty-Four

SCARLET

On Sunday morning, Ariadne came into our room holding an envelope.

I jumped up and ran over to her. "Oh my word," I said.

"What's in it?" Ivy asked, panicked.

"You don't know?" said Ariadne. She looked a little put out, but she wasn't in a flood of tears.

I put my hand on her shoulder. "Don't you worry, whatever it is. We'll help."

"Um," said Ariadne.

Ivy bounded over to us. "It's all right, Ariadne. We'll find out who's sending these, and we'll stop them."

"My daddy?" Ariadne looked completely baffled.

"Your daddy?" What was she on about?

Wordlessly, Ariadne opened the envelope and held out its contents.

It was a card with three small dogs on the front. It said, "THREE CHEERS FOR YOUR BIRTHDAY."

"Oh, Ariadne!" Ivy said. "It's your birthday?"

Our friend nodded. "I suppose I forgot to mention it, what with everything that's been going on…"

I grabbed Ariadne in a massive hug. "Don't apologize. We're complete idiots. Happy birthday!"

"I'm so sorry, Ariadne, I didn't know," said Ivy as she flung her arms around Ariadne too. "I would have made you a card, or, or something…"

"It's quite all right," said Ariadne, once we'd finished squeezing her.

"We'll celebrate," I declared. "We'll put candles in your porridge."

I wasn't allowed to put candles in the porridge. Mrs. Knight did lead the Richmond table in a round of "For She's a Jolly Good Fellow" though, leaving Ariadne red-faced and beaming. Even Penny begrudgingly joined in.

Ariadne had received a parcel from her parents on Friday, which she'd saved without opening and now unwrapped at the breakfast table. It was a set of books by Frances Hodgson Burnett with illustrated front covers: *A Little Princess* and *The Secret Garden*. I pretended to not be interested, because books aren't my thing, but I had to admit that they were pretty. Ivy and I rarely got birthday gifts from our father and stepmother at all. We were lucky if we got socks.

I decided we should have an impromptu birthday party in Ariadne's dorm. Luckily yesterday's trip to the village meant there were plenty of sweets for the occasion, even if we didn't have a cake.

We hadn't been in her new dorm yet, since it was quite a way from ours, and you weren't really supposed to go to the younger students' rooms. It was laid out for six girls with three metal bunk beds.

When we walked in, five heads popped up from the beds. "Hi, Ariadne!" they chorused.

"Hello, everyone!" Ariadne replied. She placed her new books neatly on a shelf beside the door. "These are my best friends, Scarlet and Ivy."

"Hello, Scarlet and Ivy!" came the reply.

"Ooh, twins," said one of them.

Ariadne pointed at each of the beds in turn. "This is Agatha, Evelyn, Bonnie, Franny, and Mary."

Agatha peered down at us from the top bunk. She had frizzy brown hair that she had attempted to pin into curls, *attempted* being the key word. "Are you the twins who got the headmaster arrested?"

I gaped at her. "How did you know about that?"

"Everyone knows about that," she said, grinning excitedly. "You're practically *famous*."

"Huh," was all I could say. I'd always wanted to be famous, but I hadn't expected it to be for this.

The ginger-haired girl sitting on the bed beneath her chimed in, "And Ivy got rid of Miss Fox as well! I heard you chased her down the driveway with her own cane!"

I looked at Ivy. "Erm..."

"That wasn't exactly what happened..." Ivy started, but Ariadne quickly silenced her.

"It was *brilliant*," she said. "You should've been there. Anyway, Scarlet's decided I should have a birthday party!"

There were cries of "Oh goody!" and "How jolly!" and various other annoyingly cheerful things.

"We should play hide-and-seek," said Bonnie, a bright-eyed blond girl, "or musical chairs!"

"We don't have any chairs, Bonnie," Agatha pointed out. "Or music."

❧

In the end, we settled for a game of pass-the-parcel, using Ariadne's sweets and a bunch of packing paper and string. Mary (who was very shy and had thick glasses that looked like the ends of a bottle) was nominated to look the other way and hum loudly as the "music."

It was quite childish...but fun. We'd rarely got to go to birthday parties when we were younger, so it was nice to have one here. It certainly took my mind off all the horrible stuff that had been happening recently.

At least, until Agatha brought it up again.

"Who do you think is sending the nasty letters?" she asked. We were sitting in a circle on the carpet, amid a mess of torn-up paper, all a bit too full from eating porridge and a lot of sweets.

"What letters?" said Evelyn.

"Someone's been sending these nasty letters," Agatha explained. "I heard some of the teachers got them and went *crazy*. They had a fight in the corridor!"

There were gasps and shocked *no*'s from some of the girls.

"I heard that girl Josephine got one and threw herself out of a window!" Bonnie said.

"Now hang on a minute," said Ivy, but she was interrupted by the rumor mill in full flow.

"I heard someone in the ninth grade got one and it was so shocking that she fainted," Franny said, her dark eyes wide.

Ivy's mouth was hanging open. Was that one true?

"I heard that the letters were written by a ghost who lives in the attic and watches everything we do and can walk through walls," said Mary.

Everyone stared at her.

After a few moments, Ariadne said, "Um, where did you hear that?"

Mary simply shrugged. There was a puzzled silence as everyone tried to imagine a ghost writing letters.

"The strange thing is," said Agatha, "that no one in

our year seems to have got one yet." She sounded a bit disappointed.

Then Ariadne leaned forward and whispered conspiratorially, "We have a theory about who might be behind it all."

There were a lot of gasps. Bonnie tried to hide behind a pillow.

"*Really?*" said Franny.

"Who?" asked Mary.

I grabbed Ariadne's arm to stop her. The last thing we wanted was for these girls to blab to Madame Zelda. "We're not sure yet," I interjected.

"But," said Ariadne with a grin, "we're going to find out, I promise!"

Ariadne seemed very pleased with her birthday in the end. She even got an extra helping of pudding at lunchtime. I did feel bad that we hadn't been able to get her anything, so I gave her a lot of pats on the back instead. Around the fifth time, Ivy swatted my hand away and told me to stop it.

In the afternoon, we went to the school chapel as usual, where the vicar read us a dreary sermon. At least the hymns he'd picked weren't quite so dreary, and we sang them in our loudest voices.

And we all went to bed a little happier.

Sleep was a different story though. I had nightmares

of the shadow spying on us through cracks in doors, around corners, and through holes in the ceiling. It stalked about in impossibly high heels, swooping down like a black thundercloud.

Chapter Twenty-Five

IVY

The next week began with an emergency assembly.

We all knew what it would be about. Girls bursting into tears and teachers fighting in the corridor weren't exactly easy things to miss.

Mrs. Knight didn't bother with her usual introductions. She looked frail and tired and had purple bags under her eyes as if she hadn't been sleeping. "Girls," she said, "you've all heard about these poison-pen letters. It is very important that if you receive a letter, you *do not open it.*"

Nadia put her hand up. "Any letter, Miss? Even from family?"

"Any letter," said Mrs. Knight firmly. "I will be checking all the letters that come into the school." *Ugh.* That reminded me of Miss Fox. "If someone leaves you an envelope in your room or at your desk or anywhere else, bring it to me. Do not read it. Is that clear?"

"Yes, Miss," everyone chorused.

I looked around the hall. Miss Danver and Miss Simons were absent, and I thought there might be a few more teachers missing as well.

Mrs. Knight carried on. "I have received several telephone calls this morning from worried parents. It appears they have received an identical syndicated letter."

Nadia raised her hand again, and this time waggled it about in the air a bit. "What did it say, Miss?" she asked.

Mrs. Knight paused, then said, "It was sent by someone who identified themselves only as a concerned parent. It seems to have contained details of the recent happenings at the school, and..." She took her glasses off and rubbed her temples. "It warned that Rookwood was unsafe, and said parents should remove their children immediately."

A wave of gasps rippled around the hall. What if parents actually started taking students out of school? I wondered if our father had received a letter and whether or not he would be worried. It seemed unlikely. If our stepmother had received it, it was probably a pile of ash in the bottom of the fireplace by now.

"Right," said Mrs. Knight, suddenly straightening up and pasting her cheerful face back on. "There is no need to panic. We do not believe the school is unsafe."

I glanced at Scarlet. *They don't?*

"Although I advise all girls to be vigilant, particularly where anonymous letters are concerned," she continued, "I do not think there is any immediate danger." She smiled brightly at us. "Everything will continue as normal."

Clara raised her hand, and then, as if she thought that wasn't drastic enough, stood up. Everyone turned to look at her. "What about what happened to Josie, Miss? We still don't know who pushed her!"

That caused a commotion, and several teachers had to step in and calm everyone down.

Pansy Jenson, the angry eleventh-grade girl from the stables, leaped to her feet. "What about the horses, Miss? Some of them are still missing!"

Then everyone started shouting at once.

"Quiet!" Mrs. Knight ordered. "Quiet!"

Everyone was too busy shouting about mean letters and attempted murder and missing ponies and, if Ariadne's roommate Mary was involved, probably ghosts as well. I bowed my head, put my hands over my ears, and held on to Scarlet in case she decided to jump up and join in.

Then a shout rang out even louder than the rest, in a voice that commanded the obedience of your very soul. *"Everyone will be silent immediately."*

The cries faded to whispers. Those who had stood slowly sat back down. And I looked up to see Madame Zelda at the front of the stage.

She looked coldly furious, standing in front of Mrs.

Knight, poised in her high heels. The whole school stared at her dumbly.

"Thank you," she said, in a way that implied she wasn't really thanking us at all. She had an icy exterior, but I had a notion that, somewhere inside her, a spark of fury was burning. "Remain silent while the headmistress is talking."

As she left the stage, I felt her gaze slide across all of us, and I shuddered.

Mrs. Knight was standing very still, her mouth hanging slightly open as she watched Madame Zelda descend the steps. "Um, yes," she said. "Right. All of you, enough of this poppycock about conspiracies. I'm your headmistress, and I'm telling you Rookwood School is as strong as ever! We are absolutely doing our best to investigate all of these unusual circumstances, but I'm sure it will prove to be nothing serious."

Someone coughed.

"Please write to your parents or guardians and tell them that there is nothing to fear. Rookwood is a safe and happy learning environment! Isn't that right, girls?"

Silence.

Then, at the back of the hall, someone started to cry.

∽

"Oh gosh," said Ariadne as we headed for history. "I really hope my daddy didn't get one of those letters.

He'll be panicking something awful right now. And I only just persuaded him to let me come back."

"We won't let him take you away again," said Scarlet firmly. She was swinging her satchel as she walked, narrowly missing a group of seventh graders.

"Unless you *want* to go home," I said. Rookwood wasn't truly safe, and we knew it. Scarlet and I didn't really have anywhere better to go, but if Ariadne wanted to leave, I didn't want her to feel that we were stopping her.

"Are you kidding?" she asked. "As if a little danger would send me packing!" She grinned. "I laugh in the face of danger!"

At which point another girl walked into her and sent her stumbling backward. She fell into a sitting position on the floor, mousy hair sticking up at strange angles.

"It's all very well laughing at it," I teased as we helped her up, "but perhaps make sure you're looking where you're going first?"

In history, Scarlet sat down at her old desk. She'd once left me a clue by pouring her rose perfume inside it, and it still smelt faintly of roses, even from the desk next door. Madame Lovelace hadn't yet arrived, so that meant we could chat for a while longer.

Nadia leaned over her desk. "Do you think everyone's going to leave? If my papa thinks I'm in danger, he'll turn up here any minute..."

Ariadne smiled shyly at Nadia. "My daddy is the same."

"I don't know," I said. "I don't think my parents would pay much attention. But there are some parents who will. What will Mrs. Knight do if everyone leaves Rookwood? Will it have to close?"

"Ha," snorted Scarlet. "No one was removed from the school twenty years ago when Mr. Bartholomew was dishing out terrible punishments and *murdering* people. What makes you think anyone will listen now?"

Suddenly Ariadne slammed her hand over her mouth.

"What?" Scarlet said.

"Twenty years ago—" Ariadne began.

But that was all we got out of her, because at that point Madame Lovelace hobbled into the room and the class fell into a brooding silence once more.

At lunch, we found a secluded place where Ariadne could finally explain her brain wave without being eavesdropped on. To be more exact, it was the supply closet near the ground-floor lavatories. It was full of lavatory paper and brooms, but at least it was private. We just had to hope the caretaker didn't walk in.

"It was what Scarlet said," she began. "It made me think of the Whispers, and everything that happened back then."

"What about it?" Scarlet asked.

"Well, you're trying to find out about your mother and your aunt, aren't you? Ida and Sara. One thing we know for sure is that Ida was friends with Emmeline, who drowned because of Mr. Bartholomew. So logically, wouldn't it make sense for her to be in the group that tried to bring him down?"

I nodded. "Of course! But..." I felt my face fall. "We lost the code book. In the fire. And we can't get to the wall of names."

"I know," said Ariadne, and there was a glint of excitement in her eye. "But I wrote down the names, didn't I!"

She pulled a crumpled piece of paper out of her pocket and flattened it out against her skirt.

"I nipped back to my dorm and found it. Take a look," she said. The list read:

Alice Jefferson
Elizabeth Fitzgerald
Ida Smith
Katy Morwen
Talia Yahalom
Bronwyn Jones
Emmeline Adel

There, right in front of us, was our mother's true name, where it had been all along.

Chapter Twenty-Six

SCARLET

"*I knew it!*" I cried. "I knew I'd seen that name somewhere before!" I waved my arms and nearly knocked over a bottle of cleaning fluid.

It was utterly weird, seeing our mother's real name alongside her friend's that she had stolen. Suddenly what had been a stranger's name meant everything.

"I can't believe it," said Ivy. "I mean, I *can* believe that she was in the Whispers, but I can't believe we'd seen her name before, and that we didn't realize!"

"That's not all," said Ariadne. "I thought of something else in history too. Miss Jones knows about that time, but she was only very young and doesn't remember much. But we haven't asked any other teachers, have we?"

I suddenly realized where she was going. "Madame Lovelace! She might remember Ida and Sara."

Madame Lovelace was one of the oldest teachers in the school. She was white-haired and wore big, thick, round glasses. And she was always covered in dust, though I wasn't sure if that was a side effect of being old or whether she was just clumsy when clapping out her erasers.

"I don't know how long she's taught here, but she certainly seems like a permanent fixture," said Ivy. "We have to talk to her."

When it had come to the Whispers, there were few teachers we could trust to ask about them. Mr. Bartholomew had really got his claws into everyone. But now we just wanted to know about two old students. There was no risk, was there?

I gave Ariadne a slap on the back. "Once again, Ariadne, you have proved that you're a genius." Ariadne beamed. "Let's go and find her," I continued. "Right away." I went to push my way out of the cupboard, and walked straight into a broom.

"Slow down a bit, Scarlet," said Ivy.

I rubbed my arm. "Never!"

∽

Luckily, Madame Lovelace was easy to find. She was snoozing at her desk in the history classroom.

"Miss?" I gave her a gentle poke in one dust-clad shoulder.

"Mmm?" She sat up, smacking her lips, her eyelids slowly lifting.

"You were asleep, Miss," I said.

"I was not," she replied indignantly. "I was merely resting my eyes. Now what was it you wanted?"

I was about to tell her that she was snoring, but Ivy spoke before I had the chance. "We wanted to ask you something."

"It's historical!" said Ariadne gleefully. "Well, sort of."

That caught the ancient teacher's attention. She slapped her hand about on the desktop until she found her thick glasses and pulled them on. "Ah," she said. "Ask away."

Ivy gave a shy smile. "We wanted to know if you taught at the school twenty years ago..."

Madame Lovelace proudly tapped her chest with a wrinkled hand. "Oh yes! Forty years of service. I have taught many hundreds of girls in my time."

"Do you remember two sisters? By the name of Ida Jane Smith and Sara Louise Smith?"

She squinted through her glasses as if she was trying to gaze through the mists of time. "That sounds familiar..."

"They looked a lot like us," I said, pointing back and forth between me and Ivy. "Only they weren't twins."

"Oh! Relatives of yours?" Madame Lovelace asked.

I nodded, but I didn't want to be too specific. Some things I felt you had to hold close to your heart.

She rubbed a speck of dust from her sleeve. "Now that you mention it, that rings a bell. One was older?"

"Yes," we said.

"And they probably wore pearl necklaces a lot," Ariadne contributed.

Madame Lovelace was firmly back in her memories. "I *do* remember them! Lovely girls. The younger one could be a troublemaker, but she had a kind heart."

I caught Ivy giving me a glance and then quickly looking away.

"The older one, she was a dear. She was a wonderful seamstress. If only I could sew as fine." Madame Lovelace looked down at her own drab, dusty clothes. "I remember..." she paused. "I remember having the class put on a little play about the Romans. Everyone else just wrapped themselves in a bedsheet, but she made herself a very fine toga with gold edging."

I felt a warm glow hearing about our aunt. All these things we should have heard from our own family, we were getting in glimpses at Rookwood School. "Can you think of anything else, Miss? Do you know what happened to them?"

She stared a moment longer, and then shook her head, which started off her coughing. When she finally stopped, she spoke again. "The older girl...was that Sara?" I nodded. "She wanted to make dresses. I don't know if that's what she did. The younger...I knew little about her. Or if I knew, I've long since forgotten."

My warm glow turned a little darker. Every time we got close to finding out more about our mother we seemed to get turned away. It was as if she didn't want us to know.

Ivy must have realized that we weren't going to get any more out of our history teacher. "Thank you for your time, Miss."

"That's quite all right," she replied. "Now, if you'll excuse me, I need to rest my eyes for a little longer..."

✁

We shuffled out into the corridor and shut the door behind us.

"What a waste of time," I said bitterly. "I should've known her memory wouldn't be up to scratch." I glanced at the clock. It was nearly time for class to start again.

"We learned something," said Ivy, ever the optimist. "That's better than nothing."

Ariadne stopped us. "No, listen, Ivy's right. We do have something to go on!"

Ivy looked as clueless as I felt. "We possibly have an aunt who's good at making dresses?"

"Yes," Ariadne grinned. "And you know what ladies who are good at making dresses do for a living?"

"Erm..." I looked down at my shoes. "They sell them?"

"*Precisely.*" Ariadne snapped her fingers. "Your aunt might have opened a dressmaker's shop. We might be able to track her down!"

Ivy gaped at her. "How?"

Sometimes I had a feeling that Ariadne was the real brains of our outfit, and Ivy and I were just a couple of sidekicks. I wouldn't tell *her* that though. Obviously.

"Well, when my mummy wants to find a particular dressmaker, she looks in the local directory. If Sara didn't move too far away from here, we might be able to find her." Ariadne looked very pleased with herself.

"We'll go to the post office on Saturday," I decided. "And we'll look at the directories."

We had a chance of finding our aunt, and if we had that...then there was a chance we could find out who our mother really was.

Chapter Twenty-Seven

IVY

The rest of the week brought more letters. Mrs. Briggs, the hockey teacher, apparently threw a hockey stick through a window after receiving one. I heard that some of the older girls had dutifully not opened theirs and taken them to Mrs. Knight, who put them straight in the fireplace. I wondered how their curiosity hadn't got the better of them.

On Wednesday, the first parent arrived demanding to take his daughter home. We stood on the gallery over the foyer and watched as the angry father shouted at Mrs. Knight. "It's perfectly safe!" she kept insisting. But the tiny seventh grader looked relieved as her father led her away.

There was a telephone call for Ariadne as well. We were allowed to wait in the office while she spoke.

"Yes, Daddy."

"No, I'm absolutely fine, there's really no need."

"Well, yes, some things have happened, but I'm all right! I've got Scarlet and Ivy with me."

"No, I'm not going to be pushed out of a window! I shall stay well away from windows!"

"No, you don't need to come."

"Do I need to remind Mummy about the petunias?"

"Very well, then."

"I love you too, Daddy. Good-bye."

I knew it was foolish, but I kept wondering if we would hear anything from our father. But as Scarlet kept telling me—he had never cared before, so why would he start now?

On Thursday, more parents arrived, and more girls were taken out of school. Rumors spread that one mother had been furious at the loss of her daughter's expensive pony, and that they might sue the school. Most of the horses had been tracked down, much to Rose's relief, but there were still some missing. Many parents were no longer convinced that the school could look after their horses or daughters.

On Friday in assembly, Scarlet and I received a letter from our scatterbrained Aunt Phoebe.

I tore open the envelope eagerly, and once Mrs. Knight had cast her eye over it to make sure it was all aboveboard, I began to read...

Dear Ivy,

I was so pleased to receive a letter from you.

I have found the turkey knife. It was in the shed.

I'm sorry to hear that you are anxious at school, but I'm sure it's perfectly safe. If you need me you can always telephone Mr. Phillips, and he'll come and get me. I must get myself one of these telephones, they do seem wonderfully useful.

Don't worry about Scarlet, she always finds a way to get by.

Your stepmother is still cross with me, I presume for having you both for Christmas, I'm afraid. But since your father agreed to it, I don't think there's much she can do.

I hope I will be able to see you again in the school holidays!

Your aunt,
Phoebe Gregory

I watched Scarlet as she read through it. "Hmm," she said. "No mention of anything that's happened recently here. Maybe she didn't get the letter from the 'concerned parent.'"

I was surprised that my twin didn't fly into a rage at the mention of our stepmother. We felt certain that she'd been bribed by Miss Fox to go along with

Scarlet's disappearance, and her presence in our lives was like a constant insult.

But I just replied, "Why would she though? It was probably only sent to parents."

"Hmm," said my twin again.

❦

We had ballet that afternoon, and the studio was looking emptier than usual. Scarlet was her usual twitchy self as she flitted between excitement and fear that she wasn't the best. It was silly really. She would get a good part in the recital either way, why did it have to be the main one?

But of course, she didn't see it that way. It was all or nothing. Scarlet and Penny spent most of the lesson trying to outdo each other. Whatever my sister did, Penny would try to do it higher, or straighter, or with more balance. And then Scarlet would try to do the same. I just wished we could go back to dancing for enjoyment, and not have to worry about performing.

Madame Zelda ran the ballet class with an iron fist. We all remained silent as she barked orders and told us exactly what we were doing wrong. But as soon as it was over, she always congratulated us and told us we had done well. She was as changeable as the English weather, and I missed Miss Finch's calm composure. I hoped that wherever our absent teacher was, she was doing all right, and that her leg wasn't hurting her too much.

"*Très bien*, girls. Do not forget, the auditions will be soon. I hope you are all prepared. Once we have the parts in place we will see about getting the sets and costumes." She clapped and made us all jump. "Oh, I do enjoy a performance..."

That night, the dream returned.

At first, I wasn't sure if I was dreaming or awake. I heard something outside in the corridor: heeled shoes clacking past.

I started to panic. I knew only two people who wore heeled shoes that sounded like that. And I didn't want either of them outside our room in the middle of the night. I buried my head under my blanket and prayed that the heavy desk would be enough to protect us.

Then I was back on top of the hill, standing in the green grass. Bright sunlight shone in my eyes, and I had to shield them with my hand. The shadow was there again, and she wore a dress that billowed in the wind.

I tried calling all the names I knew, and when I said "Ida" the shadow suddenly turned. But I still couldn't see its face.

It ran toward me, and just as it came closer, a gust of wind knocked me back into the grass, and I fell to the earth with a thud.

✌

I woke and peered at the moon outside. I was still in my bed. Scarlet was snoring gently beside me. And we were alone.

✌

We woke on Saturday filled with excitement and purpose. Today we would go to the post office and find the directory. Whether or not we would also find our aunt, well...that was another question.

After breakfast, we headed out to Rookwood village—a long walk down the tree-lined drive in the spring sun. There were clouds overhead though, threatening a shower at any moment. I hoped it would hold off while we made our trip.

The post office was near Kendall and Smith's. It looked like any other house in the village, except for the peeling red postbox outside and the "Post Office" sign above the door. Once you stepped inside, there was a big wooden counter with scales on, surrounded by pigeonholes. The postmaster was an old man, who was currently asleep behind the counter.

"Probably just resting his eyes," Scarlet snorted.

I wasn't sure if we should wake him, but Ariadne clearly had other ideas. She enthusiastically dinged the little bell that sat on the countertop.

The postmaster jumped out of his seat, nearly knocking it over. He brandished a ruler at us. "Is it the Germans?" he said, his eyes wide and wary.

"No, sir," Scarlet said. "I think they're all still in Germany."

He glared around the room. "You never know with the Germans."

"We've come to ask about the local directory," Ariadne said, gently steering the conversation back in the right direction. "The one for Fairbank." Fairbank was the nearest big town. "May we take a look at it?"

"Oh," the old man muttered. "Oh, right. Of course. Right this way."

He lifted up a movable section of the counter and ducked out, in a surprisingly sprightly fashion for someone who was old and had just been asleep moments ago. He led us to one corner of the post office, where there was a glass-fronted cupboard full of large books with thick black covers. He pulled down the last one and set it out on the table below.

He went to open the book, and then paused and fixed Ariadne with a suspicious expression. "You aren't a German spy, are you?"

"Not that I know of," said Ariadne.

"That's all right then." He opened the first page of the huge directory. "There you go, girls." With that, he shuffled behind the counter and off out the back somewhere.

The contents page listed an awful lot of things.

Judicial lists, sporting lists, charitable and benevolent organizations... The advertisement beside the page was for a hat shop, boasting "Mourning Millinery Always in Stock." What a depressing thought.

"Where do we start?" I asked.

"Look for Smith in here?" Scarlet suggested.

She pointed to the section labeled "General Directory: page 57."

"I hope she hasn't married and changed her name..."

We heaved the pages over until we got to fifty-seven, and then there was more heaving to get to the letter *S*. Unfortunately, there were three pages of Smiths. Scarlet groaned.

Ariadne combed through them. "Aha!" she cried suddenly. And then, "Oh..."

"What is it?" I tried to peer over her shoulder.

"There's two people named Miss Sara Smith," Ariadne said with a sigh. "And a Sarah Smith too. How do we know if any of them are her?"

Drat. I hadn't thought of that.

"What?" Scarlet groaned. She pushed Ariadne out of the way and gave a growl of frustration as she scanned the page.

Smith, Miss Sara, 2 Union Street

Smith, Miss Sara, 52 Princes Street

Smith, Miss Sarah, 16 Canal Street

"Oh, for goodness' sake." She grabbed a handful of pages and slammed them back over, making Ariadne gasp.

And then I gasped but for a different reason.

"Look! Look!" I said, pointing at an advertisement in the center of the page.

DRESSES *by* SARA LOUISE

❖ ❖ ❖

Dressmaker and Purveyor
Of Fine Clothes and Elegant Costume
BEAUTIFUL FASHIONS FOR THE MODERN WOMAN
EST. 1925

❖ ❖ ❖

52 PRINCES STREET, FAIRBANK
"Darling, don't you know? It's a Sara Louise!"

Ariadne squealed. "That's it, it must be her! Look at the address!"

"I did it!" Scarlet grinned.

"Accidentally," I pointed out.

Ariadne quickly reached into her satchel and pulled out a pen and paper. The post office had little pots of ink on the counter for customers to use, so she dipped her pen and began copying down the address. "This is *brilliant*," she said. "Now all we need is a way to get there..."

"And an excuse," said Scarlet.

But just as she said that, I saw an excuse right there on the page.

Now it was my turn to grin. "I know what we're going to do," I said.

Chapter Twenty-Eight

SCARLET

Ivy's idea was a good one. In fact, I wished I'd thought of it myself and felt slightly miffed that I hadn't.

It was still before noon on Saturday, so we had plenty of time. The only problem was that now we had to find Madame Zelda. I didn't even know if she came to the school on weekends.

We searched everywhere for her at Rookwood, but there was no sign. I supposed she probably stayed at home, unless she was off plotting crimes, which I couldn't rule out.

So, when we ran into Mrs. Knight in the corridor, I decided she would do. In fact, I had a bit of an idea.

"Morning, Miss," I said as we approached. "Madame Zelda has asked us to do something for her..."

Ivy swatted at my arm, but I ignored her. I had a feeling a lie would work better than the truth.

"What would that be?" said Mrs. Knight. She looked completely flustered, as was usual lately. I felt that would probably work to our advantage.

"She wanted us to go and look at some costumes for the *Sleeping Beauty* performance," I lied. "There's a shop in Fairbank she wants us to go to." I snatched the piece of paper from Ariadne's hands. "Here, she gave us the address."

Mrs. Knight glanced down at it. "Oh, right," she said. "Have you got the bus fare?"

"I have," said Ariadne. "And I memorized the timetable from the village."

Mrs. Knight frowned, but then she said, "Do you have a chaperone?"

I was about to lie about that too, but Ivy shook her head. *Ugh.* My twin really doesn't know how to play along, sometimes.

At that moment, a tall girl with dark hair and a pointed nose walked by. She was wearing a shiny prefect badge, pinned to her school tie.

"Ah, Elsie," called out Mrs. Knight, "please chaperone these girls to Fairbank today. They need to look at some costumes."

I groaned inwardly. How were we going to talk to Sara Louise properly now?

Elsie plastered a big smile across her face. "Oh, absolutely, Miss. I would *love* to." She leaned forward and pinched my cheek. "These little ones are just *so* sweet!"

I held my breath and tried very hard not to slap her.

"Very well then. Be back before five, please," Mrs. Knight said. As she hurried away, I wondered how many more parents had threatened to take their daughters out of school.

As soon as our headmistress had disappeared, Elsie's overenthusiastic smile faded, and she made a sound like "ugh" under her breath.

She started examining her nails. "Well? What are you waiting for?"

"Um, you?" I said.

She looked up at me, radiating sarcasm. "If I'm going to be your nanny for the day, you could at least try to be a little less irritating."

I raised my hands at her in the universal gesture for "What?"

"Ugh," she said, much louder this time. "Come on. Don't make me wait for you." And with that, she strode off in the direction of the foyer.

"What a—" I started, but Ivy slapped me before I could say anything too rude.

"She doesn't seem particularly pleasant," said Ariadne diplomatically.

We followed Elsie out into the foyer (where the front desk now had a sign that read "Secretary temporarily unavailable—please proceed to Mrs. Knight's office") and out of the front doors of the school. The prefect marched ahead of us toward the village, but then took a sharp left at the crossroads just before we got there.

I hadn't been on a bus many times in my life, and honestly I was quite surprised to find there was even a stop so close to Rookwood—given that it was in the middle of nowhere. I had a suspicion it was something the school didn't want any of the students to find out about, in case they made a run for it. I guessed Mrs. Knight thought we were in no danger of escaping, since we had a prefect with us.

The bus-stop post was half-hidden in the hedge with just the top of the sign sticking out. There was nowhere to sit, so we just stood by it while Elsie tried her best to look like she wasn't with us. It was windy, and my tie kept whipping out from my dress and hitting me in the face. I realized Elsie had pinned her prefect badge there to stop it doing just that.

"Ooh, bus!" said Ariadne after a while, pointing down the road.

It was painted yellow and brown and chugged along the road slowly toward us. I hoped it wouldn't go that slowly the whole way, or it would take us *years* to get to Fairbank.

Elsie hopped aboard. "Tickets for one adult and three children to Fairbank, please," she said to the conductor, bringing out that sickly sweet smile again.

Children? I stuck my tongue out at her for that. The conductor just smiled and tipped his hat before tearing off the four tickets. Elsie pulled out a purse from her pocket and handed him the fare.

The bus was nearly empty—the only other passengers were an old woman and a man with a briefcase. I went straight for the back, hoping Elsie would stay away from us. But as I sat, Ivy and Ariadne plonking down beside me, she appeared right in front of us.

"All right, pay up," she said.

"What?" Hadn't she just paid for the tickets?

"I'm not paying for your little excursion," she said, looking bored. "Someone give me the pennies, or else we're getting off."

Ivy was frowning at her, but Ariadne hurriedly pulled out her own purse and retrieved some coins. "There you go," she said, her face resigned. Elsie nodded and then walked back to the front.

I turned to Ariadne. "What did you do that for? You didn't have to pay her! She's being a complete wretch!"

"Sorry," said Ariadne, blushing. "I just panicked."

⚮

The journey was long and winding, with green countryside eventually fading into the Victorian terraces that marked the edge of the town. I stared in delight. I hadn't seen a town in so long! Especially since...well. You know. Being locked away. I tried to put that thought out of my head.

"It's not very clean," said Ariadne, wrinkling her nose. The buildings we were passing were blackened with smoke, and there was litter blowing in the gutters.

It got a little tidier as we neared the bus station. It wasn't much more than a hut with "Motor Coach Station" painted on the sign and spaces for a few buses to park. As the bus pulled in, there was a whooshing noise and strong smell of fumes.

I wasn't surprised when Elsie hopped off ahead of us. "How are we going to lose her?" Ivy asked. "I don't know how we're going to talk to Sara with her hanging around..."

"I say we push her under a bus," I said, though I didn't entirely mean it.

We needn't have worried. As soon as we'd thanked the conductor and climbed down from the vehicle, Elsie turned to us and said, "You know where you're going, then?"

I didn't exactly, but there was a map on the wall nearby. I pointed to it. "I'm sure we can find our way, since we're not *stupid*."

She didn't catch my tone. "Fine then. Be back here by four or I'll box you around the ears."

And with that, she'd walked off, humming to herself.

"Perfect," I said. "Fifty-two Princes Street, here we come."

It was in the center of the town, only a few streets away from the bus station. We turned a wrong corner at one point (Ivy's fault), but we corrected it and managed to find ourselves on the right street. Though unfortunately, it was the wrong end (Ariadne's fault).

We headed down, counting the numbers. "Thirty-four, thirty-five, thirty-six..." I chanted aloud.

"We're getting close!" said Ariadne excitedly.

"Forty-seven, forty-eight..."

And then, finally, we were there. Number 52.

The sign was painted a deep blue and peppered with stars, the proud name of "Dresses by Sara Louise" standing out in swirling white writing. The tall windows boasted the most beautiful dresses in spectacular gold and yellows that stood out against the dark backdrop like the stars in the night sky. The tops of the windows were filled with matching stained glass, and over the doorway was a crescent moon, glinting in the sunlight.

A tiny sign on the door read "Open."

"Wow," Ivy and I said at the same time.

"Gosh," said Ariadne.

And at that point, I decided to panic. "What if she's not there?" I said. "Or what if she is, but she doesn't want to see us? What if she hates us?"

Ivy looked at me, her expression cool and level, though I could feel her fear underneath. "Only one way to find out," she said.

◇

A little bell tinkled above the door as we stepped inside the shop. It was a bit dark, but just as beautiful as it had looked from the outside. It was filled with dresses and tutus and cloaks and all manner of clothing. I could see silks and lace and cashmere. I longed to touch them all. But we had a job to do.

There was no one at the counter. The shop was silent, motes of dust spiraling in the light from the stained glass. I took a deep breath, and Ivy slipped her hand into mine.

"Hello?" I called. "Anybody there?"

A velvet curtain behind the counter rustled and was pushed aside, then a lady stepped out. "Welcome to Dresses by Sara Louise, may I help you?"

She was tall and pretty, and her perfectly curled dark hair was going gray at her temples. She wore an elegant deep red dress with puffed sleeves and a satin bow and short fingerless gloves over slender fingers.

And she was also wearing a pearl necklace.

She looked at me. And then she looked at Ivy.

And then she said, very politely, "Oh my..."

And fainted.

Chapter Twenty-Nine

IVY

We dashed behind the counter.

"Miss? Are you all right?" Ariadne kept saying. "Miss?"

The woman's eyelids fluttered. She moaned quietly and put her hand over her forehead. "Ida?" she murmured. "Am I dreaming?"

And with a rush of emotion, I knew that we'd done it. We'd found our aunt!

It took Sara Louise a few minutes to come around. We were crouched by her, Ariadne fanning her with a pamphlet, when she finally came to and sat upright.

"Oh," she said, reaching out and gently touching my face. Her skin was soft. "Am I seeing a ghost? Can it be?"

"You're Sara Louise Smith, aren't you?" I asked, my voice shaking. I could already feel my tears threatening to spill. "Sister of Ida Jane Smith?"

She nodded. Then she turned her head a little and took in Scarlet beside me. "And seeing double as well..." she said. Then she blinked. "Oh, girls, I'm dreadfully sorry for fainting on you." She climbed to her feet gracefully and hurried over to the front door of the shop. She turned the little sign from "Open" to "Closed."

"That's quite all right, Miss—" I started.

"Come out into the office with me. We must talk." She pulled back the velvet curtain and waved all three of us through.

At the back of the shop was a smaller room with filing cabinets on one side and shelves of fabric on the other and a writing desk at the back. There were several dressmakers' dummies, each stuck with numerous pins. There were two wooden chairs in the center, and Sara fetched another two from the corner of the room.

As we took the seats, she sat in front of us, leaning on a gloved hand. "I can't believe it," she whispered. "I just can't..."

"Miss, we're—" I started.

"I know who you are," she said, and her eyes clouded over. "I knew the second I saw you. And I know those uniforms. Please, before we take this any further..." She reached out and took my hand. "Is she alive? Is my sister alive?"

My heart wrenched. I felt like the bottom was falling out of our world.

It wasn't so long ago I'd said those very same words. But incredibly, wonderfully, *unbelievably*, my sister *had* been alive. She was lost, but I had found her.

How could I tell this woman, tell our aunt, that her sister was gone forever?

My head spun. I stared down at her hand, and I clutched it back tightly. "I..."

Scarlet found the words for me. "We're so sorry," she said, and I'd never heard her sound so sincere.

Sara leaned back in the chair and closed her eyes. "I'd hoped..." she started. "I'd dared to hope. But really, deep down, I think I knew."

We sat in heavy silence until eventually she shook her head, and the clouds disappeared from her eyes.

"I'm sorry, girls. Let's start again, shall we? Please, tell me your names." She looked questioningly at Ariadne, who gave a shy smile. "And your friend?"

"Scarlet and Ivy," my twin said. "And this is our best friend, Ariadne."

Sara smiled brightly and said, "How wonderful to meet you. How truly wonderful." She shook us all gently by the hand.

I was in awe. Our family had never been the best. We had a wicked stepmother, a father who was uncaring and absent, and sweet Aunt Phoebe who was mainly absentminded. How could this beautiful, independent woman be related to us? She seemed unreal somehow, as if she'd stepped out of a painting.

Sara took a deep breath and exhaled shakily. "Please, tell me everything," she said. "What's happened in your lives? How did you find me?"

Scarlet and I exchanged a glance. Where on earth to begin?

I told her, as gently as I could, how our mother had died shortly after we'd been born. That we were mirror twins, a perfect reflection of one another. I told her about Father and how he'd looked after us well to start with, though he'd had a fiery temper, and then how he'd gone cold as ice when he married our stepmother, Edith. I told her how they'd sent us away, Scarlet to Rookwood School and me to live with our Aunt Phoebe, Father's sister.

Scarlet and Ariadne joined in, as we tried to summarize everything that had happened since I'd been summoned to Rookwood. Sara's eyes were getting wider and wider. There were a lot of gasps and *no*'s and *really*'s as we explained how I'd had to impersonate Scarlet after Miss Fox had had her locked in an asylum, and how Ariadne and I had tracked down her whereabouts with the hidden pages of her diary.

And then we explained what had happened last term with the return of Mr. Bartholomew. Our aunt's eyes went dark. "*Him*," she said.

I talked about how we'd found out about the Whispers, and how we'd used everything we knew to prove that the headmaster had drowned a student in the lake.

"After all these years," Sara said. "He was finally caught. If only it had been sooner..." She shook her head again.

"There's more," I said. "After that, we went looking for the memorial for the girl who drowned. And we found it...but it said the name *Emmeline Adel.* The name that we'd always thought was our mother's."

Sara nodded slowly, saying nothing.

"And we had to find the truth after that," said Scarlet. We'd been batting sentences back and forth like a tennis match. "So, we talked to our school librarian, because she'd been at Rookwood when we thought our mother had been there, and she showed us this school photograph."

"And we spotted our mother immediately," I continued, "because she looked just like us. And she had the pearl necklace that I inherited." Sara's hand unconsciously moved to touch the string of pearls at her neck. "But then we saw you in the picture, and we realized that she must have had a sister too."

"And then?" said Sara, fascinated.

"Miss Jones tracked down your names for us," Ariadne said. "And once we knew that, we asked Madame Lovelace if she remembered you."

"Ha!" exclaimed Sara. "She's still there? My goodness, she must be ancient! She was elderly when she taught us, or so I thought..."

Ariadne grinned. "She remembered you all right, and that you'd been a great seamstress who wanted to become a dressmaker. We hoped that you might have achieved your dream, so we tracked you down in the directory."

Sara sat back in the chair, putting her gloved hand to her mouth. "You girls," she said finally, "are the most wonderful detectives." She looked at all three of us in turn. "You are so brave and so clever, and I'm *honored* to meet you."

I felt a warm glow start to burn in my heart. Her words were melting the ice that had covered me for so long, shut away in Rookwood School and so rarely ever hearing a kind word. Scarlet was grinning like a Cheshire cat, and Ariadne looked like she was about to cry.

"It's an honor to meet you too, Aunt Sara," I said, trying very hard not to cry myself.

She smiled at me, though her smile was coated with sadness. She'd found two nieces, but she'd also lost a sister, however long ago that had been.

"Now," she said. "I must tell you the truth about your mother."

Chapter Thirty

SCARLET

I had waited all my life to hear about our mother. And now finally, finally I was going to know the truth. And it was, as Ariadne would say, *brilliant*.

"We were very close," Sara began. "The very best of friends. I loved my sister dearly. But at Rookwood... things changed. I was older than her, and so we were separated. She befriended Emmeline, and soon they seemed closer even than we had been. Emmie could be a troublemaker, but it was Ida who would get the trouble. Emmie would get away with anything, because she was a prefect."

Ariadne gasped. "She was the double agent!" She turned to me and Ivy. "The Whispers' code book—it was a prefect notebook, wasn't it?"

"So, Emmeline was the prefect all along!" I said.

"Yes," said Aunt Sara. "And Ida would follow her

anywhere, she admired her so. And then Emmie started the secret group—the Whispers. Ida was forbidden to tell me about it, but she let some details slip. Emmie was horrified by what she'd seen as a prefect, and she was determined to take down Headmaster Bartholomew.

"But he was worse than she'd imagined. One day, Emmie was finally caught doing something she shouldn't have been doing. And she must have confronted the headmaster, because he pushed her into a terrible punishment. Ida told me that he forced Emmie to swim in the freezing lake. And Emmie, she wasn't a strong swimmer. He wouldn't let her out. He wouldn't let her stop. He let her drown."

"Ida told you this?" I asked. "Did she...witness it?" I felt furious all over again, remembering what Mr. Bartholomew had done.

"I don't know for sure," Sara said, "but she knew enough. Ida loved Emmie, and she'd long hated Mr. Bartholomew. It completely broke her. There was nothing I could do. She was devastated beyond belief."

I searched Ivy's face and saw the sadness in her eyes. I knew that was how she'd felt when she thought I was truly dead. I quietly reached out and took her hand.

"Her grief..." Sara continued, twirling a button on her dress and staring into the distance. "It drove her off the rails. I tried to stop her, but..." she sighed. "All she wanted was revenge against *him*."

I nodded. I knew that feeling too.

"After what happened next, I never saw her again."

We gasped.

"It was only in her letters that I learned what had truly transpired." Sara got up and went over to the writing desk and clicked open the drawer.

I felt my hopes rising. "You still have the letters?"

"I do indeed," said Sara, rifling through the drawer. "They have kept me going, through these years, building everything for myself. When she first disappeared, I had no way of knowing what had happened. I was terrified. The first letter was an enormous relief, despite the contents. Aha!" She pulled out a sheaf of yellowing papers, tied with a red ribbon, and brought them over to us.

"What did they say?" asked Ivy, completely rapt.

Sara stared down at the little pile. "Ida tried to confront the headmaster. Or perhaps that's not quite strong enough—she tried to physically *attack* him, screaming that she knew what he'd done. He overpowered her and threatened her. Told her if she ever breathed a word of this, he'd hunt her down and make her life miserable no matter what it took. She managed to get free, to run. After that...she knew there was no going back. She'd have to face the police, or the headmaster himself, and she didn't know which was worse."

I squeezed Ivy's hand hard. Our mother...I hated that she'd been in that situation. I hated that she hadn't *won*. And I had that tiny bit of pride that, all these years later, we'd won for her.

Ariadne was nodding along with what Sara was telling us. "So, Ida went on the run. But then why on earth did she take her friend's name? Why steal Emmeline's identity?"

Sara shook her head. "It wasn't like that. Ida said that she made it as far as London and tried to find lodgings. She thought she might be able to get by as a maid. But when she was asked her name, she panicked and realized she couldn't use her real one. So, she said the name that had been constantly on her mind." Sara held up the letters, and I longed to reach out and touch them. I bit my lip. "This was on the doorstep of a wealthy man. He ended up taking pity on her and employing her in his staff, and so she had no choice but to become Emmeline if she didn't want her past to be found out."

"And she managed it?" I asked. It was crazy to think that our mother had pretended to be her friend, just as Ivy had pretended to be me. History really did repeat itself.

"Yes," said Sara. "She lived in London for several years. I would occasionally receive letters from her, but there was never a return address. She made me swear not to tell our parents where she was, because she thought they would turn her in."

"She was probably right," I said. "You can't trust parents."

"I *like* my parents," said Ariadne, pouting, but I ignored her.

Sara chuckled a little. "Whether it was the right thing to do or not, I don't know. If only life would tell us when things are right or wrong." She frowned momentarily. "So, your parents...your father," she continued. "Ida met him in London, at a party held at the wealthy man's house. It wasn't quite love at first sight—in fact, I think he positively annoyed her initially."

I grinned. I could imagine.

"But they soon got along like a house on fire. And then she fell for him. I never met him, but the way she would talk about him in her letters...it was true devotion. Ida—your mother, she didn't like many people, but when she loved, she loved intensely." Sara smiled a sad, sad smile, like the weight of the past was bearing down on her. "Your father persuaded her to move with him to the country, to the village where he came from. He'd inherited a house from his father. At first, she was horrified, knowing it was close to Rookwood. She was so afraid she'd be recognized, even though years had passed. But she couldn't explain that to him, as he knew nothing of her past. And, like with Emmie, she would follow him anywhere."

I tried to imagine Father showing anything other than rage or cold indifference. It was too hard.

"But you didn't find her, even then?" Ivy asked.

"I wish I had," said Sara. "But she truly didn't want to be found. She made me swear to never go near her as long as the headmaster still lived. She thought he'd come after me if he saw we were in contact, that he'd hurt me to get to her..." She stopped and swallowed. "I knew that she was somewhere near Rookwood, but where...I didn't know, and I couldn't find out if I was going to respect her wishes. She would've been mortified, and I didn't want to lose her twice."

"And the letters?" I asked, waving at them. "There was nothing to give you a clue?"

"She wouldn't risk any clues," our aunt explained. "She mailed her letters from different places, so that the postmark would vary. She married your father, and though she hated deceiving him, she thought she had no other option but to keep living as Emmeline. I kept her secret for her, and I waited all my life for Mr. Bartholomew to die. I always hoped that if I stayed near here, one day I might just bump into her, in the street..." Sara's voice cracked a little.

Ivy reached into a pocket and handed her a handkerchief.

"Thank you," our aunt said, and just held it in her hands.

For a few minutes we sat there, saying nothing, trapped in the past. I wondered if Sara had exhausted everything she had to say about Ida. But then she began again.

"When the letters stopped," she said, "at first I barely noticed. I could never write back to her, after all, and her correspondence was sporadic at best. I thought it had been a long time since I'd heard from her, and before I knew it, it had been over a year..." She twisted the handkerchief between her fingers. "I feared that something must have happened to her. It wasn't the sudden shock of hearing that someone is gone. It was slow and dark and insidious. But there was worse to come..."

"Worse?" I asked.

She looked me straight in the eye, and her own eyes shone with tears. "Worse somehow than the fear that she'd died, was the fear that she'd forgotten me. That she'd stopped caring. That she'd left me all alone in the world."

My vision blurred as tears sprang to my eyes.

"But you're here," she said, and she took my hand and Ivy's, and held them closely. "And your names..."

A tear rolled down my cheek, and I looked at Ivy, and a matching mirror tear was sliding down hers.

"She named you Scarlet and Ivy," Sara said, and now she was truly crying, "like we were Sara and Ida. S and I together once more. *She never forgot me.*"

Chapter Thirty-One

IVY

It took all of us a while to stop crying. Even Ariadne was sobbing into her handkerchief.

"Aunt Sara," I finally said, "we never...we never knew Ida, or Emmeline, or whatever she wanted to be called. And I always worried...that perhaps she never cared, because..."

I couldn't get the words out.

"Because no one ever has," said Scarlet, and she stood up, and I could sense the built-up anger pouring off her. "Not our father, not our stepmother, and *certainly* not the teachers at Rookwood. No one sees us. We're just *girls*. Girls who should dress nicely and stay quiet and do as we're told. They don't *care* about us."

"Scarlet," I said gently. I didn't want her to go into a rage, but I couldn't deny that I felt everything exactly as she said it.

"It's the truth!" The tears streamed down her red cheeks. "They tell us what to do. They find a way to lock us up. Whether it's in a school, or an asylum, or when they marry us off to some rich man, they find a way. Why would our mother want us? Nobody wants us, Ivy! Nobody—"

Sara put a hand on her arm, firmly. "Scarlet," she said. "I think you both need to read this."

Scarlet froze, her chest heaving, as our aunt pulled at the red ribbon on the pile of letters, letting it fall away. She took one from the bottom of the pile and handed it to Scarlet.

My twin sat back down. The paper was shaking in her hands. The handwriting...our mother's. It had to be. I'd never seen it before, but I knew.

"This is the truth," Sara told us. "This is how she felt."

Together, we read our mother's final words to her sister.

Dearest sister,

I hope this finds you well. It has been so long since I last wrote! How things have changed since then. I have grown bigger than ever. I am quite convinced it is to be twins, but the doctor says otherwise.

It is harder to move around now, and I keep trying to persuade Mortimer that we need a new housemaid, for though he dotes on me so he could not wash a shirt or darn a sock to save his life, and I want to put my days of maid work long behind me. Oh, but how I love that foolish man!

And sister, I'm beginning to think I must wipe my slate clean. Being with child. . .it changes everything. I cannot bring life into the world with the weight of my secrets dragging me down. I intend to tell Mortimer the truth, and I pray that he will love me no less. It would mean the world to me if you could meet him once the air has cleared. But even more if you could one day hold my children.

Do I regret what happened, all those years ago? I do, truly. Though my cause was noble, my actions were not. I should not have taken a name that was not mine to take. I should not have run from my fate. It cost me my family, a price far too high. I lost you, my dearest friend.

But every mistake, every trauma, every wrong footfall has led here. Happiness is blooming out of the ashes. Life finds a way.

My love grows with each day that passes and I feel as though my heart can barely contain it. Could it be twin girls, dear sister? They might be just like us. Whether one child or two, I know this: they will be special, and they will be loved.

And there I must leave you, for now. The sun is setting and my husband will soon be home. I will darn socks by candlelight and dream of my clean slate.

Until we meet again.

Love, always,
Ida

All this time. All the tears we'd cried for the mother we'd never known. Every lonely moment that had passed throughout our childhood. We'd thought no one had cared. We'd truly believed it.

Our mother had cared.

She had loved us.

Suddenly that was all that mattered.

"Thank you, Aunt Sara," I choked.

She smiled gently. "It means the world to me to finally meet you."

"We'd love to get to know you..." I started.

But that was when Ariadne looked at the clock. "Oh my gosh!" she cried. "We have to go, or we'll be late for the bus, and Mrs. Knight will kill us!"

If Elsie doesn't kill us first, I thought.

I stood up. "I'm so sorry," I said to Aunt Sara, wringing the pleats of my dress in my hands. "We've only just met you and we have to leave again."

She stood up too, so tall and elegant. "I'll write to you both," she said. "I don't think I could ever go back to Rookwood, after everything, but...you are welcome to visit me again."

I wasn't sure if we'd be allowed to visit again, especially if our excuse about looking for costumes was found out to be a lie. But that gave me an idea. "We're going to be in a ballet recital in the Theatre Royal, here in Fairbank. Would you come and watch?"

Our aunt smiled widely. "I would like nothing better," she said.

We ran from the shop, praying we wouldn't miss the bus.

"I can't believe it!" Ariadne kept panting as we jogged in the direction of the bus station.

"Me neither," I said. Scarlet stayed silent, but there was a glint in her eye.

We arrived at the bus station to find Elsie with arms folded and feet tapping. "Where have you been?" she yelled.

"Busy doing what we said we were going to do," Scarlet said with a glare. She held out Aunt Sara's costume catalogue—a stroke of genius from Ariadne, who'd realized we ought not to go back empty-handed.

I'd wanted to tell Sara about everything that had happened recently at Rookwood, but there had been no time.

"You're late," Elsie snapped. "We nearly missed it, you little weasels. Now get on."

She climbed aboard the chugging bus and we got on behind her, Scarlet pulling faces the whole time.

Elsie sat as far away from us as possible, much to everyone's relief, and we spent the bus journey talking about everything we'd found out.

The words ran through my head, over and over.

We have an aunt. We know the truth about our mother. Our mother loved us.

That last thought was so big, it was like it was enveloping me, wrapping its arms around our little group. I felt like no matter what happened next, that thought would somehow protect us.

The problem was, I had no idea what would happen next. And things were about to get much, much worse.

Chapter Thirty-Two

SCARLET

I was still so elated from meeting Aunt Sara, I could barely spare a thought for anything else.

While Ivy was taking a bath, I did something I hadn't done in a long while: I wrote in my notebook, the replacement for my diary, which had long since been ripped to pieces and scattered around Rookwood.

Sitting at our desk, I took out my ink pen, and I started to write.

Dear Diary,

You won't believe what has happened! We have finally learned the truth about our mother.

We tracked down her sister, our Aunt Sara. She was incredible and beautiful, and she has her own shop. She told us everything.

Our mother was just like us. She tried to fight

the headmaster, and it backfired terribly. So, she was forced to go on the run. And that was when she took her friend's identity, quite by accident.

And more importantly than that...

She loved us. We weren't always unwanted.

I held my pen above the page, just staring at that last line I'd written, and a drop of ink splashed down on to it.

And then a shadow fell across the page.

I looked up to see the door of our room wide open, and Penny standing over me.

I snapped the book shut and jumped to my feet. "What do you want, witch?"

She glared down her nose at me. "What are you writing? It wouldn't be one of those *letters*, would it?"

She was such an idiot. "This is a notebook. It has lines." I shook the thing in front of her face. "It's not even the same paper the letters were typed on."

"Hmmph," she said, tossing her hair over her shoulder. "I *know* you're involved somehow. Though I have to say, I thought you were better than this."

I stepped closer to her. "Firstly, that's a lie. You've never thought I was better than anything. Secondly, I thought you'd given up on being a hideous beast. Is that not the case?"

She stepped closer herself, until we were almost nose to nose. "Don't try to take me on, Gray. You'll lose."

I almost laughed in her face. "This isn't really about

the letters, is it? You just don't want me to beat you to the starring role in the recital."

She turned away, her ginger hair whipping around. "You haven't heard the last of this. Oh—" She looked back. "And you should keep a closer eye on your sister."

And then she marched prissily out of the room. Moments later, Ivy appeared. "What was that about?" she said, adjusting the towel wrapped around her head.

I sat back down again, but I didn't stop glaring in the direction Penny had gone. I had no idea what she was on about. "Penny's competing in the local witch contest," I said. "Trying to see who can be the ugliest and most poisonous."

"Oh," Ivy replied. "Well then. No contest."

✖

I barely slept that night as I couldn't stop thinking about it all. What had our mother done to Mr. Bartholomew? Had she been scared when she'd run away? How had she kept up her secret for so long?

When I did sleep, I had a familiar nightmare—I was up on the roof of Rookwood again, staring down from the dizzying height. Only this time there was something *off*. I wasn't frightened, but I had this pressing sense that someone was standing behind me, watching over me.

I woke up sweating and blinked in the light. "Ugh," I said, pulling my pillow over my head.

It was Sunday, which meant chapel. The pews were looking emptier than usual, and we didn't have to shuffle up to fit people in. The vicar's monotonous voice echoed off the walls.

I probably should've been listening, instead of just doodling in my notebook. I dished out a fair few glares. One for Penny, one for Elsie Sparks, who I hoped we were never forced to go anywhere with again, and one for Ivy, because she kept slapping me for the doodling.

At the end of the sermon though, the vicar said something that made me prick up my ears. "Mrs. Knight informs me that more cruel letters have been, mmm, received," he said. The vicar was ancient, and everything he said was in a drone. "I just want to remind you girls, mmm, that we must do unto others as we would wish to be done unto us."

"More letters?" Ariadne whispered. "When will this end?"

"We must, mmm, remember," the vicar continued, "to not pay any attention to any of these ill-written letters." He shuffled his papers on the lectern, and an envelope slipped out and spiraled to the floor.

Every single eye in the chapel fell on that envelope.

"Mmmhmm." The vicar coughed, suddenly going very pale. He reached down to pick it up, his back creaking as he did so. "I shall be, erm, handing this in to Mrs. Knight too..."

❧

The gossip blazed through the remaining girls in Rookwood. So-and-so had got a letter and handed it in to Mrs. Knight. Whatsername's parents had had her transferred to another school.

The usual torrents of girls through the corridors were becoming more like streams. Several girls had lost their roommates and were too scared to stay on their own. And everyone was on the lookout for the next poisonous letter.

Mrs. Knight was stubbornly maintaining her "The school is a safe place" blissful ignorance.

And then dinnertime came.

We lined up while the grumpy dinner ladies spooned out the usual slop. "I don't suppose we could have something other than stew?" I asked one of them. "I mean, some cake, maybe? With ice cream?"

The cook leaned over and brandished a ladle at me. "If you want to go 'nd buy it 'nd make it for yourself, Miss Gray, then you can. We're 'avin' last night's leftovers. Now shut up and move along."

Pulling a face, I picked up my tray and headed over to the Richmond table with Ivy right behind me.

We sat down next to Ariadne. "We should thank Miss Jones," she said.

Ivy nodded in agreement.

"Gosh, I'm starving," said Ariadne and started tucking into her stew. I stared down at my plate.

Why did it *always* have to be stew? I mean, sometimes it was called roast dinner, or some other form of meat with potatoes and what might be some vegetables if you squinted at them sideways. But when you got right down to it, it was basically always stew. I sighed.

"Bluuurp," Ariadne suddenly hiccupped.

I looked up. Ivy had an uneaten forkful halfway to her mouth and was staring at Ariadne.

"I don't feel well..." Ariadne muttered.

I looked down at the stew. "It's not *that* bad, is it?"

Ariadne was turning slightly green. "I really don't feel well." She went to stand up, but her arms wobbled. And, like she was in slow motion, Ariadne slumped forward over the table.

There was a mighty *crash* as her plate and glass fell to the floor, spilling their contents.

"What the—" I started, and then I heard groans begin to echo along the table.

"I feel *weird*," Penny said, and her stomach grumbled loudly. "I don't...*argh!*" Her chair flew back with a screech, and she ran from the room.

Nadia was clutching her stomach, her face drawn.

The stew, I thought. *Something's wrong with the stew.*

I jumped to my feet. "Ivy, you didn't...?"

She threw down her fork and shook her head frantically.

The groans got louder. They were spreading. More people started to sway.

And, one by one, girls fell at their tables like dominoes.

Chapter Thirty-Three

IVY

Not even Mrs. Knight could talk her way out of this disaster.

The leftovers had been there overnight...perhaps it was just food poisoning. But Scarlet and I immediately suspected otherwise.

We guessed the truth: someone had put poison in the stew.

There was widespread panic. Not everyone had eaten it, but many girls had. Doctors were called. Some girls were taken to the hospital, some to their homes, and the sick bay was full for days. The poisoning seemed to vary in severity depending on how much each person had ingested.

I couldn't believe how lucky Scarlet and I were to have not eaten it. I'd been so close to putting that spoon to my mouth.

The question was: Who was responsible?

Ariadne was confined to the sick bay, and we visited her each day—along with her dorm-mates. Agatha brought her daisy chains and grapes, and Mary fetched countless books from the library for her.

It wasn't long before Ariadne's father arrived—that funny little man who reminded me of a bespectacled owl. It was Tuesday lunchtime, and Ariadne was propped up on her pillows looking a little brighter.

Her father bustled into the sick bay, this time looking more like a worried pigeon.

"Oh, Ariadne, my pumpkin!" he cried as soon as he saw her.

She groaned. "Daddy, you didn't need to come."

"Oh, yes I did," he said, waggling a finger at her as if she were a naughty three-year-old. "For pity's sake, they told me you'd been poisoned!"

"I'll be quite all right," said Ariadne. "I'm feeling much better already." She sat forward as if she were about to jump out of the bed, but then thought better of it. She glanced at me, her face red with embarrassment.

"My little princess," said her father. He tucked the sheet right up to her neck. "Your mother and I feel you simply *must* come home."

"Um," I said, hoping to get a word in edgeways. I knew there was no way Ariadne wanted to leave now, even if half the school had been poisoned, but maybe she would be safer at home.

But this time, she spoke up for herself. "I absolutely

won't." She pushed the sheet back down and straight-ened the collar of her nightgown. "I'm not a princess, and I don't need rescuing, all right?" Her expression was determined, if still a little ashen.

"But, darling—" her father started.

"*No*, Daddy," she insisted. "I'm not letting you shut me away again. My friends need me. That's all there is to it."

And, much to my amazement, he listened. I'd thought she would have to bring up the petunias again.

He took a step backward, clutching his hat in his hands. "Well...if that's what you really want, pumpkin. But you must get someone to telephone us immedi-ately if there's any more trouble, do you hear?"

"Yes, Daddy," she replied wearily.

"I'll look after her," I promised.

He smiled down at me. "Thank you, Irene." I hadn't the heart to correct him. "Such kind friends you have, Ariadne."

He said his good-byes and then was shown the way out by Nurse Gladys, who was completely frantic with the unexpected workload.

Ariadne grinned. "I'm still here," she said proudly.

I smiled back, but I felt fearful inside. Was it truly safe for Ariadne to stay at Rookwood? Was it safe for any of us?

The story reached the local newspapers. The front-page headline read **SCHOOL POISONING DECIMATES STUDENTS**.

It was the last straw. There were lines of motor cars all along the school drive as distraught parents came to pick up their daughters. You could barely go outside without choking on exhaust fumes. I wondered if Father would turn up, but I wasn't surprised when he didn't.

We watched as Mrs. Knight stood in the entrance hall, desperately trying to reassure parents that the situation was being handled.

In the absence of Miss Flit, Miss Jones had been temporarily put on secretary duty. One time as we went through the foyer, she appeared to be gently hitting her head on the desk. I didn't know who was manning the library, but I had a suspicion it would be Anna Santos.

And then Violet's guardian turned up. He was a large man with an expensive, tailored suit and a rugged beard. We watched him haul Violet out of her dorm room, kicking and screaming. He kept insisting that he just wanted to keep her safe. "Huh," said Scarlet as we watched. He hadn't even noticed when Violet had been locked in the asylum along with Scarlet. His "care" for Violet was clearly questionable. Rose was inconsolable at the loss of her roommate and protector.

I began to wonder what would happen if enough

girls were taken out of school. Would Rookwood shut down? Would the rest of us be left here while the numbers fell and fell?

I'd wanted to write to Aunt Sara, but Scarlet talked me out of it. She said that as we'd only just met her it was too much to ask—that Aunt Sara had specifically said she hated the idea of coming to Rookwood School, filled as it was with painful memories. We didn't want her to think we were asking to be rescued.

Though I wondered if we'd regret that. Perhaps we did need to be rescued.

∝

There were distractions though, as always. Just when we thought things had finally tipped over the edge, real life kept flowing on like a river.

"What else can we do?" Scarlet kept saying. "Lock ourselves in our room and never come out?"

It was a tempting possibility. I'd been afraid to eat a bite for days following the food-poisoning incident.

But you couldn't stay afraid. You couldn't let it stop you from living your life. You just had to be prepared to fight when the time came.

The biggest distraction was the upcoming auditions for *Sleeping Beauty*. Scarlet was still after the starring role.

Ariadne pointed out how strange it was that the recital was still going ahead, what with all that had happened. But Mrs. Knight was determined, despite everything, to keep our spirits up. She had become the living, breathing version of the motivational posters on her office walls. *Win your way with a smile!*

The auditions were to be held in the school hall on Monday afternoon, after a final practice of our routines. We each had to perform a small section from the ballet in front of the judges. Madame Zelda was the head judge, and she'd roped in Miss Bowler for her general sporting knowledge. Mrs. Knight was too busy dealing with furious parents to take part—many of them were now withholding fees, if they hadn't yet had their daughters removed from the premises altogether. Madame Boulanger stood in her stead, although she didn't have any qualifications apart from supposedly being French.

We lined up outside the hall in our tutus and tights, toe shoes in hand. The line was much shorter than I'd expected, especially given that there was a ballet class for every year.

Scarlet wasn't so much queuing as practicing. Even without her shoes on, she was warming up and trying desperately to get each position perfect.

Penny was making sure her hair was flawless in its tight bun. Scarlet and I had gone for matching red ribbons wound around ours, borrowed from Ariadne.

"Still practicing, I see," said Penny smugly. She leaned back against the wall, arms folded. "Of course, you need it, don't you?"

She nudged Nadia, but her best pal just rolled her eyes and looked away.

Scarlet carried on dancing. "Oh, and doing your hair is going to help you how?" she said. "Want to look your best when you lose?"

"I don't lose," Penny snapped.

∾

One by one, the girls in front of us disappeared through the doors. My twin was shaking, but she was trying very hard to pretend she wasn't.

"I'm going to the lavatories!" she announced suddenly and darted away. She'd picked the worst time to leave: Nadia had just been called in, and I was left alone in the corridor with Penny.

I turned away, hoping she wouldn't notice, but of course I had no such luck.

"Well, well," she said, leaning into my face. "This is it."

"What?" I asked.

"The moment when I win *my* part. And your sister isn't going to stop me." She smiled, revealing her pointy white teeth.

"She's just going to do her best, Penny," I said. "It's not up to her who wins. It's up to the judges."

Without warning, Penny lunged forward and ripped the bow from my hair.

"Ow!" I cried. "Penny, what are you—"

She dangled it in front of me. "Wouldn't it be a shame if Scarlet were to find out I'd been picking on you?" she hissed. "She'd be furious, wouldn't she? Maybe furious enough to go crazy and lose any chance of ever winning the role? Furious enough to get herself kicked out of school altogether?" She danced over to the window on the other side and lifted the latch, pushing it wide open. She held Ariadne's ribbon out and watched it flutter in the breeze.

"Don't," I warned, but she'd already let go of it.

"Oops," she said, putting a hand over her mouth. "We'd better not tell her then, don't you think?"

The hall door opened and someone called, "Next!"

Penny winked at me, and pranced daintily into the hall.

I stood still, fists clenched, chest feeling tight.

And then Scarlet was back, returning to her place in front of me. "I'm all right," she said, uncertainly. "Everything is fine." She took a deep breath, and then stared at me. "What happened to your hair?" She waved her hand over my messy bun. "And where did your ribbon go?"

I swallowed. *You promised*, my mind said. *You promised no more secrets.* But I couldn't risk Scarlet losing the only thing that was keeping her sane. "Nothing happened," I lied. "I just decided I didn't like how it looked."

"Hmmph," my twin said. "Now we don't match." But she didn't press it any further.

We waited in silence while Penny auditioned—the familiar piece of music flowing from within the hall.

Finally, the door opened again, and Penny walked out. She had an even more self-satisfied grin than before, if that was possible. "Good luck being better than me, *Scarlet*," she taunted.

"Next!" called a loud voice from inside.

Scarlet turned a very strange shade of pink. "You go first," she said suddenly to me, as Penny strutted away down the corridor.

"What?" I stared at my twin. "But..."

"No buts," she said, her eyes wide. "You first."

And then she pushed me into the hall.

❧

I stood there at the bottom of the stage, blinking in the bright lights, my heart in my throat and one loose strand of hair tickling my neck.

"Ah, Ivy Gray." That was Madame Zelda, her familiar but slightly strange voice reaching my ears. "Welcome. Take the stage, please."

I looked around as I sat on the first step and laced on my shoes. There was a table set up before the stage, with Madame Zelda in the center. To her left sat Miss Bowler, and to her right Madame Boulanger. There were a few girls sitting behind, watching—a mix of those who had already auditioned and some ballet students from the higher grades—but most of the seats were empty.

So, who's on the piano if Madame Zelda is judging? I looked over, only to feel myself groan inwardly. It was Elsie Sparks, the grumpy prefect. She gave me a patronizing wave.

I felt a pang of sadness, deeply missing Miss Finch. Was she ever coming back?

"Get on with it!" Miss Bowler yelled, her hands cupped around her mouth.

Shaken out of my haze, I took a deep breath...

Don't fall, Ivy. Don't make a fool of yourself in front of everyone.

...and climbed the steps.

Chapter Thirty-Four

SCARLET

In that moment, the audition was all that mattered.

I barely registered Ivy when she peered out of the hall and told me I was on. She looked relieved.

After I'd laced on my toe shoes, I climbed up to the stage, and felt the music flow through me.

I was Aurora. I was a beautiful princess, dancing in a palace. I was anywhere but Rookwood. Anyone but Scarlet Gray.

It was everything I'd practiced for. Seconds before I'd entered, Penny's words were ricocheting in my head. Now they were gone, replaced by the movements. Madame Zelda was right: it was all about control. I controlled my mind; I controlled my body.

As the music came to an end, I felt myself slowly coming out of the trance. Someone was clapping.

I blinked and looked down to see the judges in front of me.

"Bravo," said Madame Zelda. She was standing up and applauding. "That was wonderful, Scarlet. Well done."

I beamed.

"Miss Bowler, Madame Boulanger—what are your thoughts?"

"Oh well," said Miss Bowler, dragging herself upright. "Good job, I say. Very nice." It was unusual to hear her say anything that wasn't bellowed.

"Erm, it was...how you say...very excellent," the French teacher added. "It was definitely ze ballet, I tell you that. *Très bien.*" She wasn't any better at pretending to know about ballet than she was at pretending to be French.

Madame Zelda sat down, running a hand through her strange silver hair. "Thank you, Scarlet. You may go."

I climbed off the stage, buzzing. *I did it! I did it!*

I went over and sat next to Ivy, who took my hand. I wanted to jump up and down, but perhaps that was a bit premature.

Madame Zelda stood up again and turned to face everyone. "Thank you, girls," she said. "The parts will be allocated tonight, and the list will go up first thing tomorrow. It will be posted on the bulletin board in the foyer. Remember, you have all displayed excellence today."

I grinned. Penny was glaring at me, which made everything even better.

ℒ

The next morning, I woke up early, before the bell had even rung. While Ivy was still sleepily dragging a comb through her hair, I was up and dressed and running out of the room. "Wait!" she called after me, but I had to get to that bulletin board.

A small group had formed around it already in the near-empty hallway. I pushed my way through, not afraid to use my elbows.

But just as I was getting to the front, Penny shoved me aside, heading in the opposite direction. Her expression was deathly sour.

No, surely... Did I?

I elbowed a few more people out of the way, until finally I could see the list.

And there it was, in black and white:

Princess Aurora: Scarlet Gray

"Yes!" I cried.

I got a few glares, but I couldn't have cared less. I scanned the rest of the list. Many of the main parts were taken by the few older girls who had auditioned, some of them playing more than one role. And I spotted that Ivy had won the part of the Diamond Fairy. Nadia was the Lilac Fairy.

And what I saw next made me unsure if I should laugh or cry.

Prince Florimund: Penelope Winchester

Penny had scored a lead role after all. But it was the role of the *prince*. My prince. She had to play my love interest.

Oh, dear Lord.

I looked back and saw her leaning against the corridor wall, her face like thunder.

"Oh, Penny," I jeered as she shot me a glare. "Didn't you know you couldn't ever be a princess?"

Her chest rose and fell rapidly, and her nostrils flared. Her fists were shaking. "You'll regret this," she said.

Others were staring and giggling now. "What's wrong, Penny?" I stepped closer. "Don't you want to kiss me and wake me from my slumber?" I made a pucker face and watched as her cheeks went crimson.

She moved even closer. "Maybe you're the one who needs to wake up," she snarled. She shot out an arm and pointed. "Because you haven't seen what's happened to your twin *right under your nose.*"

I looked at where she was pointing. Ivy was standing there, and her mouth dropped open.

"Ivy...? What's she on about?" I asked.

"Scarlet, it's nothing, you don't need to—" Now Ivy's face had gone red.

"Lying again, are we?" said Penny. "You won't even tell the truth to your own sister."

"Ivy?" I said again. The other girls all turned to look at my twin.

She stared at her feet. "Please, if I tell you, you have to promise not to make a scene."

"I'm not promising anything," I shouted. "What's going on?"

Ivy took a deep breath. "Penny's been bullying me whenever you're not around. She—"

There was some sort of explanation that followed this, but I didn't hear it. Because at that point I'd jumped on Penny Winchester and was wrestling her to the ground.

"*You witch!*" I screamed. "You utter *witch!*" She tried to get away, but I grabbed her hair and pinned her to the floor. "You apologize to my sister *right now!*"

"You shouldn't have taken *my part!*" she yelled back at me and slapped my face, hard. And then she shoved me backward across the hard floor. "You shouldn't have taken everything from me!" People were cheering us on. Then Penny was coming at me, her fist raised to hit me again...

Suddenly I felt a firm hand pull me up by the back of my dress, and I staggered backward. Mrs. Knight had hold of me, and she did *not* look happy.

"Both of you," she said. "My office. Now!"

Mrs. Knight sighed and took off her glasses.

"Tell me again why you thought it was appropriate to *fight each other*, girls?"

I was glaring at the carpet. It was that or look at her motivational posters, which seemed to be judging me. "She started it. She bullied Ivy."

"Is this true, Penelope?" Mrs. Knight asked.

Penny sniffed. "Oh no, Miss. I did nothing wrong. Scarlet just attacked me for no reason."

Mrs. Knight ran her fingers along the desk and said nothing for a few moments. "Why do I find that hard to believe? Penelope, if Scarlet attacked you for no reason, why were you trying to punch her?"

"Because..." Penny swallowed. "Because she's the one who's behind all this! She poisoned everyone to get rid of the competition! I bet that's what happened! You should search her room!"

My mouth dropped open. "Don't be so ridiculous," I said. "You just pulled that out of thin air! I had no way to poison the stupid stew. And besides, Ivy and I nearly ate it ourselves!"

"But you didn't," Penny pointed out. "You didn't get sick!"

"Neither did lots of other people," I said. "It doesn't prove anything."

Mrs. Knight took her glasses off and rubbed her

nose. "Scarlet, I don't really believe that you had reason to poison everyone. But you have to understand that we need to take these accusations seriously. Girls have been hurt. If you have any idea who's behind this, then…"

"Well," I retorted, "have you asked Madame Zelda?"

Mrs. Knight went bright red. "Madame Zelda is a respected teacher at this school, Scarlet! Kindly keep *those* kinds of accusations to yourself."

Penny gave me the smuggest look in history, and I fought the urge to punch her. "How do you know it wasn't her?" I asked, pointing an accusatory finger. "She's covering for herself by blaming me!"

Mrs. Knight opened her mouth to say something, but now Penny jumped in first. "You're pathetic! Utterly pathetic! Don't bring me into this when I'm innocent!"

"You're blaming me just because you *lost* to me! When will you accept it? I'm better than you at ballet. I'm better than you at *everything*!"

I knew I was being over the top, but it was the only way you could get through to an idiot like Penny.

She jumped to her feet. "You know what?" she hissed. "I wish you *had* been poisoned."

"Girls, that is quite enough," Mrs. Knight shouted, but we'd gone too far to stop now.

"They should've given you an extra helping of the stew," I growled back at Penny, "so we could get rid of you forever."

"Oh, that is *it*!" Penny yelled, and she shoved my

chair so hard that it tipped over backward, and I flew toward the floor...

And landed at the feet of Madame Zelda.

"What is this?" she demanded from the open doorway. I looked up, dazed and upside down. Her hands were clamped on to her hips.

I tried to say something, but I'd hit my head and everything was jumbled. Penny was frozen, hovering over me, fist raised.

I tipped myself upright, my brain suddenly registering how bad this situation was. *Oh no...*

Madame Zelda was red with fury. "I will not have my best ballerinas brawling like alley cats. This is a *disgrace!*"

"Miss," Penny started, quickly painting her innocent face back on. "It was just..."

Our ballet instructor ignored her completely. "Mrs. Knight," she said. "Do I have your permission?"

Mrs. Knight nodded wearily.

"This behavior will not be tolerated," said Madame Zelda. She pointed at us in turn. "Scarlet Gray. Penelope Winchester..."

I blinked hazily, dreading the imminent blow.

"...you are hereby *banned* from performing in the recital."

Chapter Thirty-Five

IVY

I had never seen Scarlet so miserable.

She was devastated, hurt, and embarrassed beyond belief. And though I mostly blamed Penny, I also blamed myself.

"You should've told me," she whispered as we lay in bed that night. "We said no secrets." I could hear the cracks in her voice.

I wanted to apologize, but I couldn't find the words. "I know," was all I could say.

To make matters worse, Scarlet had not only been banned from performing in *Sleeping Beauty* but also from attending ballet lessons until the recital was over. I practiced my part as the Diamond Fairy with the others while my twin stayed in room thirteen and moped.

She barely ate—though that was understandable, given recent events—and she didn't want to talk to anyone. Not even Ariadne's offer of a midnight feast cheered up Scarlet. "I had enough of staying up all night last term," she said with a huff.

And Rookwood School itself was in even more of a state. Hundreds of girls had been taken away by their parents. Even sweet Dot Campbell had gone for a "holiday," and we suspected she wouldn't be coming back. Soon there wouldn't be many of us left.

On Friday, Mrs. Knight called a late afternoon assembly. "Girls," she said, followed by a long pause. "Once again, I would be grateful if you could reassure your parents and guardians that nothing is wrong. The ballet performance of *Sleeping Beauty* is to take place next week as planned. We would like to invite all families to come along. This will be a chance to show what Rookwood School is *really* like!" Her voice echoed in the cavernous hall.

I wasn't sure if showing what Rookwood was really like was exactly what she wanted. Especially since it tended to include things like poison and murder.

"We need to *stick* together!" Mrs. Knight said, and about two people cheered. The rest of us stayed quiet.

"Stick," said Scarlet suddenly. "Stick! Oh my God!"

"That's right, Scarlet!" said Mrs. Knight. But Scarlet had jumped up and was already running from the hall.

∾

As soon as assembly finished, I found Ariadne. "What's Scarlet up to?" Ariadne asked. I grabbed her arm and pulled her along.

"No idea. She just flipped." I looked down at my friend's clothes. "No hockey gear?"

"Canceled," she managed. "Not enough players. Miss said I couldn't play attack and defense at the same time. Where did Scarlet go?"

"I don't know that either!"

We ran through the empty corridors, searching for my sister.

And when we got to the door that led down to the ballet studio, it was wide open. I looked at Ariadne. "You don't think..." I started, but we both thought it. We hurried down the stairs.

The chilly studio was empty. I rubbed my arms. But there were noises coming from the office at the back. "Scarlet?" I called.

The door swung open, and my sister appeared, holding out a walking stick.

"*Look!*"

"Scarlet, what?" I asked. "What's going on? How did you get in there?"

"There's more than one way to snoop on Madame Zelda, dear sis! And Ariadne taught me a few things about lock-picking," she said. "But that's not the point. Look at Miss Finch's stick!"

We stepped closer, and I peered at it cautiously. And to my horror I saw that there was a dark stain on the wood.

I put my hand over my mouth. "Oh no," I said. "Oh no."

Ariadne looked horrified. "Somebody hit her with it?"

Scarlet nodded, her eyes burning with anger. "*Somebody*. Somebody who took the stick away after I saw it. Somebody who hid the evidence *in her office!*"

Ariadne grabbed at her mousy hair. "No, it can't be..."

I felt sick. Miss Finch really was in danger. The hidden message in her letter had been real!

And just as I thought that, Madame Zelda came down the stairs.

❧

"Miss Gray?" she said sharply. "You aren't supposed to be down here. You are banned from ballet."

I grabbed my twin's arm. "Scarlet, don't," I tried, but she shook me off.

"It's not about *ballet*, Miss," my twin said, stomping across the studio floor. She held out the walking stick like a weapon.

I shared a worried glance with Ariadne.

Madame Zelda had her ballet shoes on, rather than heels, but she was still far taller than us. "I won't have any insolence," she warned, tapping her long fingernails on her hips.

Scarlet mirrored the teacher's stance. "I need to ask *you* some questions, *Miss*," she said.

Our ballet teacher's eyes narrowed. "Oh? And what would they be?"

"Why did you do it? Why did you do all of it? You got rid of Miss Finch, didn't you? You hit her over the head with her own walking stick and you left her somewhere, *didn't you*? Because you hated her, and you wanted her job! Is she even alive, Miss? And that wasn't enough for you, so you set out to destroy the school! You let loose the horses, and you pushed Josephine out of the window, and you sent those nasty letters, and you poisoned the stew!"

Madame Zelda gasped, but didn't say a word. *Oh no!* Hadn't Scarlet learned her lesson about confronting teachers?

Scarlet stood there, chest heaving. "Say something!" she yelled, "Admit it!"

"Wait," said Madame Zelda, holding out her hands. "I didn't... Why would you think...?"

I thought I'd better step in with some logic. "We found Miss Finch's walking stick in your office. And you suddenly appeared when she disappeared," I explained. "You basically said that you had a rivalry with her. And, well, you're the only new and mysterious person in school, and—"

"There was a letter that spelled out *help me*," Scarlet interrupted. "The telephone call supposedly from her could have been faked, couldn't it, Miss? Another woman putting on her voice. And now this! Her walking stick with *blood* on it!"

"Something's happened to Rebecca?" Madame Zelda asked.

"And," Scarlet interrupted, "you lock your office and sit in there typing, no doubt crafting your poisonous letters. You've got something to hide, I know it!"

I shot my twin a look. If Madame Zelda was innocent, we were going to be in massive trouble.

But to my surprise, our strange new ballet teacher sat down heavily on the piano stool, and put her head in her hands.

"You've got it all wrong," she whispered.

"Sorry?" said Ariadne.

When she lifted her head, there were tears in Madame Zelda's piercing eyes. "I'm not here because I wanted to hurt Miss Finch, or anyone else. I'm here because I wanted to make amends. But I am doing an absolutely terrible job of it."

My twin and I shared a glance. *Amends? For what?*

Madame Zelda sighed deeply, looking away into the wall of mirrors. "This wasn't how I wanted it to go. I had it all planned out..."

"Are you confessing?" Scarlet asked, suddenly puzzled.

"No! No..." our teacher said. "Or, well, yes. In a way. I suppose I have to. I..." She paused. "I had no idea Rebecca was in trouble. I thought she just left her stick behind, so I put it away for safekeeping. I was supposed to be making up for things, and I haven't done one bit of good. All I've done is taken her job!"

She slammed her fist down on the keys of the piano, the sudden noise making us jump.

"Miss," I said warily. "What are you saying?"

She fixed us with those piercing eyes. "I came to Rookwood to try and make amends with Rebecca Finch, because I ruined her life."

It was our turn to gasp. Scarlet dropped the stick, and it hit the floor with a clatter.

"But she was already gone when I arrived," Madame Zelda continued. "And when I told Mrs. Knight who I was, she presumed I was applying to cover the position. I should've corrected her, but...when I heard that Miss Finch had gone away because her...because her leg was too bad, I just thought..." She quickly wiped away a tear. "I thought I'd failed, and there was nothing I could do. So, I thought I would teach you girls, and make you the best that you could be..."

She trailed off again, but she couldn't leave us hanging there.

"You..." Scarlet started. "You ruined her life? What did you do?"

Madame Zelda was silent for a long, long time.

And then she quietly said, "I pushed her off the stage. I was the one who broke Miss Finch's leg."

Chapter Thirty-Six

SCARLET

I was horrified. I wanted to slap her. To scream at her. To do *something*. But Madame Zelda looked so pathetic, hunched over on the piano stool.

"I was young and stupid. I didn't realize she'd be so badly hurt. And now I just want to tell her that I'm sorry," she said. "I need to make up for what I did..."

"I'm not sure if you can," said Ivy. Her tone was harsh, but her face was gentle. "It's affected her whole life. You can't undo something like that."

"If there was any way..." Madame Zelda replied.

The *something* I'd been searching for came to me then. But it wasn't to lash out, as I'd expected myself to do. "I think there is a way you can help her, Miss. If she's really been abducted, we need to find her. And you can help us."

She looked up at me, the shame painted all over her face.

"I'm not saying it would make up for anything," I waved my hand as my anger started to cool, "but if she's in trouble, we need to save her."

"I don't know..." Madame Zelda started.

"It's important, Miss," said Ariadne. "If you know something—"

"I don't!" she cried. "I wish I did!" I felt myself deflate with disappointment. But then the ballet teacher carried on talking. "As I told you, she was already gone when I arrived. Mrs. Knight received a letter in the post while I was in her office; a letter saying Rebecca was taking time off. It was postmarked from the village, so I just thought she'd gone to stay nearby. But I went around every house asking for her, and no one had seen a thing. I typed up endless apology letters, but nobody had an address for her. I thought it was a lost cause."

"So, it was apology letters we heard you typing?" Ivy asked.

Madame Zelda nodded. "You can check the wastepaper basket in the office if you like. It's full of the foolish things."

"Wait a minute." There was a thought forming, and I tried to catch it before it escaped. "*Wait a minute.* The envelope was postmarked from *Rookwood village*?"

"That is correct," Madame Zelda confirmed. "In fact, well, I...I picked up the envelope when Mrs.

Knight wasn't looking. I thought it might help me to find Rebecca."

"But that means...Miss Finch is—or at least was—somewhere nearby." I looked at Ivy and Ariadne, who were nodding.

"But she's not in the village," Madame Zelda said. "I checked everywhere."

"Where else is there?" Ariadne asked. "There's the village and the school, but I've not seen much else for miles around."

I shrugged. But I'd picked up on something else that Madame Zelda had told us. "You kept the envelope, Miss? Do you still have it?"

She reached down and pulled up a large black handbag. She unbuttoned a pocket at the back of it and pulled out an envelope.

She held it out to me. The back had been torn open. The address of the school was in Miss Finch's handwriting.

Ivy looked at it over my shoulder. "If Miss Finch didn't write this of her own volition...then did someone force her?"

And then I noticed something else. There were some lines peeking out of the top of the envelope. "What's this?"

Madame Zelda frowned. "I don't know. I thought it was just scribbles. Perhaps she was testing the ink."

Perhaps not. If Miss Finch had been forced to write this letter, could she have left another clue for us? I

tore the fold of the envelope downward so we could
see the whole thing.

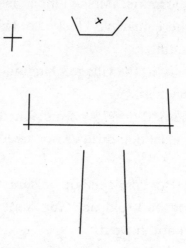

"I have no idea what that is," I said. "But I think it's
something."

Ivy turned to Madame Zelda. "Thank you, Miss. If
this is a clue, we might be able to find her."

Our ballet teacher held up a hand. "Don't thank
me," she said. "I've done too much damage."

I couldn't disagree. "You have, Miss. But maybe we
can go some way toward making it right."

❦

We left Madame Zelda to her guilt. I'd been expecting
her to be a poisoner and an attempted-murderer, but
her confession had come out of nowhere.

Ivy rushed to get an early dinner before her ballet

rehearsal. I ought to watch, to support her, but...I was too angry.

Losing my dream role hurt. I felt pathetic and sad. And I was certainly at least a little to blame for acting so stupidly. I blamed Penny even more, but at least she was as miserable as I was after losing her part too.

I suddenly felt a little more affinity with Madame Zelda. *Would I push Penny off the stage if I had the chance?* I left that question hanging in the air. I didn't want to know the answer.

I had to think about something else instead. Making everything right. Finding Miss Finch, finding the culprit.

So, at dinner, with more disgusting leftovers, we looked over the envelope again.

"Is it a stick figure?" I asked, turning it sideways and upside down to see if it would reveal its secrets.

"It looks a bit like a circuit diagram," said Ariadne. "But it's not joined up."

I had no idea what she was talking about. "Can you keep it, Ariadne? See if you can figure it out?"

"Of course," said Ariadne.

I didn't go and watch the rehearsal in the hall. Instead I had a chilly bath. Usually in the evenings, the bathrooms would be full of girls jostling for the sinks, but it was quieter than ever. When I'd brushed my teeth, I went and lay in bed feeling sorry for myself. I was missing out on all the fun.

Ivy came back later, tired but happy. "It went really well," she said, without me asking. I just grunted at her, but she was too pleased to notice. "I didn't fall over once!"

I still said nothing.

"You should have come, Scarlet. They actually ordered costumes from Aunt Sara's and they're really beautiful. And some of the remaining twelfth graders have painted this amazing castle for the scenery..."

"All right," I said, staring at the ceiling.

My twin came over and poked me in the arm. "Come on. We have to have something to distract us."

I frowned at the ceiling. "Who's taken my part?"

"One of the older girls. She's really good though."

I picked up my pillow and slammed it over my head. "Great. Just great. I hope you all had an *amazing* time while Miss Finch is out there being *kidnapped*."

"Scarlet!" Ivy gasped. "We're trying to find her! Don't take this out on me. And besides, she wasn't 'kidnapped.' She isn't a child."

"Sorry," I mumbled from beneath the pillow. I could feel my anger bubbling away beneath the surface. Then I sat back up. "Do you believe her? Madame Zelda, I mean?"

Ivy frowned. "I think so. It was truly awful what she did, but I think she wants to make up for it. I don't think she's behind all of this."

I scrunched my pillow against the wall. "But that's just it. If she isn't, then *who is*?"

My twin looked back at me, and suddenly I saw the fear behind her eyes. "Scarlet," she said eventually, her voice shaking. "I've been trying to tell you all along."

And I realized, far too late, what she was getting at.

"There's only one person who could possibly do this. Only one person who could be so cruel, and so cunning, and so *devious...*"

"No," I said. "No, no, you can't..."

"*Miss Fox*," Ivy said. "Miss Fox is *back*."

Chapter Thirty-Seven

IVY

Scarlet seemed frozen in shock. All those times she hadn't believed me, hadn't *wanted* to believe me.

"It all adds up," I said quietly. "The sounds in the night. Taking back her horse. Terrorizing the whole school. And she's Miss Finch's *mother*. She wouldn't want her own daughter getting in the way..." I swallowed.

"It can't be true," said Scarlet as a tear rolled down her cheek.

My brave, impetuous sister was deeply afraid, more than anything, of facing the very person who'd locked her away in an asylum. And I didn't blame her for one second. I was afraid for all of us. And especially for Miss Finch. Miss Fox wouldn't have hurt her, would she? I closed my eyes and tried desperately not to think about it.

I sat down beside Scarlet and wrapped my arms

around her. "I don't even know if I'm right," I said. "But if I am...we'll stop her. We'll save Miss Finch. I promise."

"How?" Scarlet asked in a low voice. She hated to be seen crying. Hated it when she wasn't being the strong one. "You can't fight her. You just can't."

"I don't know," I whispered.

Feeling shattered, in more ways than one, we lay silently back on the bed and stared up into the dark.

∾

We were woken the next morning by frantic pounding on the door.

I dragged myself out of bed and pulled the heavy desk back, enough to open the door a crack.

"I figured it out!" Ariadne whispered excitedly through the gap.

"Come in!" I said, suddenly feeling wide awake.

Scarlet clambered out of bed to help me move the desk. Ariadne bounded into the room. She was already fully dressed and had her satchel slung over her shoulder. "It's not a stick figure or a diagram," she said once I'd shut the door behind her. "I think it's a *map*."

"A map of *what*?" Scarlet asked, sitting back down on the edge of her bed.

"Of Rookwood," Ariadne said. She turned to me. "You remember when I first came here, I memorized all the maps of the school?"

I smiled. "You knew every inch of Rookwood."

"Well, yes, look." Ariadne held out the scribbled drawing for us to see.

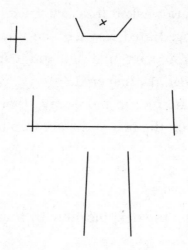

She pointed at each part with a pen from her satchel. "That big bit in the middle, I'm fairly certain is the school. The two lines at the bottom are the drive."

"And the crosses?" I asked.

"I thought at first they marked two places," Ariadne explained patiently. "But now I think the top left one is a compass, and whatever the other thing is, it's north of the school."

I squinted at the piece of paper. "There's lots of things over there. The stables, the swimming pool, the playing fields..."

"I don't think Miss Finch is likely to be in the swimming pool," Scarlet said. I ignored her unhelpful comment.

"Neither do I," said Ariadne, taking Scarlet a little more seriously than I had. "I think this mark is farther

THE DANCE IN THE DARK

away. And I remembered, from my map-memorizing...
there is something up there."

Now she took an actual map from her satchel and
unfurled it on my bed. It was of the school and grounds.

"I got this from the library," she said. "Miss Jones
was really pleased that she'd helped us before, and
she let me take this out."

I said a silent thank-you to Miss Jones.

"Up there?" Scarlet asked, leaning forward. At the
very top of the map, there was an unusually shaped
building with six sides.

"It's a hexagonal lodge," Ariadne explained. "From
back when the school was an old house. Miss Jones
said she thinks it's been locked up for years."

I tapped the sketchily drawn map. "This bit at the top
has three sides. I think she was trying to show us the
lodge! If someone made her write that letter, perhaps
she scribbled this drawing while they weren't looking."

Scarlet jumped up. "If Miss Finch is being held
captive..."

She didn't have to fill in the blanks.

"But..." Ariadne looked back and forth between us.
"Breakfast. And lessons. We'll get into trouble."

"Ariadne!" Scarlet snapped loudly. "This is Miss
Finch's life we're talking about! Who cares about
breakfast and lessons?"

I had to admit that right now I didn't, but Ariadne's
words made me stop and think. "We can't just run over
there alone," I said. "We don't know who will be there."

"We should tell a teacher," said Ariadne, still wobbling a little.

"*Come on,*" said Scarlet. She was pulling her shoes on before she'd even started on the rest of her uniform. "Since when do we tell a teacher?"

"We don't," I said, picking up her crumpled uniform and tossing it at her, "and then bad things happen."

I looked down at the end of Scarlet's bed and saw her ballet shoes discarded underneath.

"Madame Zelda!" I cried.

Scarlet and Ariadne stared at me. "What?" they both said.

"She wants to make up for what she did to Miss Finch, doesn't she? Well, let's *let* her. Let's ask her to take us to the lodge. If she agrees..."

"We won't get in trouble because we're with a teacher," Ariadne mused.

Scarlet frowned. "I don't trust her. How do we know she wasn't lying?"

"We don't," I said. "But do we have another choice? Unless you want to try asking Mrs. Knight..."

Scarlet's brow furrowed even deeper. "Fine. If she stabs us in the back, don't blame me."

"I won't," I reassured her. "Come on. Let's go."

✣

We checked the dining hall first, and then the ballet studio. Thankfully, Madame Zelda was down there, with a small group of older girls practicing for the recital.

We went over to a quiet corner where Ariadne showed her the map and explained what she'd told us.

"Will you help us look, Miss?" I asked.

Madame Zelda's face was cloudy for a moment. Then she said, "I think I must." She turned to the dancing girls and raised her voice. "Ladies, please continue. I'll be back later. Don't forget the timings for today." She tapped a long nail on a sheet of paper pinned above the piano.

2:00 p.m.—Load buses with sets and costumes
3:00 p.m.—Buses leave
4:00 p.m.—Arrive in Fairbank
5:00 p.m.—Set up theatre; final practice
7:30 p.m.—Performance

According to the clock we'd passed in the hall, it was only 8:30 a.m. Thank goodness we'd caught Madame Zelda early.

She led us out through the back doors of the school. It was bright, but the rain was beginning to fall. A rainbow hung in the sky, shimmering, before the clouds descended and it began to turn dark.

"Come," she said, beckoning to us, and then began sprinting down the path. She was wearing heeled boots—a little more practical than her normal high-heeled shoes, but I still marveled at how fast she moved. We dashed after her, buttoning our coats as we went. There was no time to waste.

If Miss Finch was in the lodge...would she be hurt? Would she be...alive? My fear fueled me, and I ran through the rain, feet crunching the gravel.

No matter what happens, I told myself, *you have your twin and your best friend beside you.*

I heard the reassuring sound of Scarlet's steps seconds behind mine. Ariadne was panting with the effort of running. We were out past the swimming pool now, on to the freshly mowed playing fields. Beyond that were the woods. I'd never been out this far before, never had reason to. Madame Zelda was some way ahead of us, her silvery white hair streaking out behind her. My own damp hair was beginning to stick to the back of my neck.

We made it across the field and ducked under the trees. The smell of wet leaves and moss filled the air and I saw fresh hoofprints in the soil.

"How far is it?" I gasped.

"I don't know!" Ariadne called from behind me. "It can't be much..."

And then she stopped, because ahead of us, Madame Zelda had skidded to a halt. The rest of us caught up, Ariadne leaning on her knees and trying to get her breath back.

"Wow," Scarlet said.

We were near the perimeter of the school, and there stood the lodge. It was built from the same stone as the school, old and gloomy gray. It almost looked like a tower—two stories tall, with a pointed roof and Gothic arch windows. The rain pattered on the slates and spilled over the edge. The windows were blacked out from the inside. It was surrounded by a crumbling, ivy-topped wall, in which sat an old wooden gate. Someone long ago had added a "Keep Out" sign, which was half hanging off.

"How long...has this...been here, I wonder?" Ariadne managed.

"Looks like forever," said Scarlet.

"Let us go," said Madame Zelda. Apparently not one to be deterred by a sign, she gave the gate a swift kick and it groaned open.

We followed her in, and I stared up at the lodge. One side was covered with green ivy, and vines were trying to creep in through the roof. "It doesn't look like anyone's been here in years," I said, hearing the worry in my voice.

"Ah," said Madame Zelda. "But yet..." She put her hand on my shoulder and guided me over to the threshold. It was a stone slab, thick with dust, but there were...

"Footprints?" I said.

"And..." she leaned closer, and sniffed the door handle. She certainly wasn't getting any less strange. "Oil. Someone's oiled this handle recently."

I glanced at Scarlet. That was a sign, for certain.

Madame Zelda tried the handle, but the door stayed

shut. It seemed to be locked. She said something in a foreign language I didn't recognize, but it didn't sound very polite.

"It's locked?" said Scarlet. "Now what are we going to do?" She kicked a bit of the wall, and the stone crumbled away. The lodge looked so frail we probably could've dismantled the whole thing piece by piece.

"Um," said Ariadne. She raised her hand.

Madame Zelda turned to look at her. I think we all wondered why she was raising her hand when we weren't in a lesson. "Yes?"

"I'mquitegoodatpickinglocksMiss."

Our ballet teacher frowned. "What was that?"

Ariadne took a deep breath, and repeated, "I'm quite good at picking locks, Miss. Sorry, Miss."

Madame Zelda's expression unexpectedly brightened. "Give it a try then!" she ordered.

Ariadne stepped closer and peered at the lock. "Aha," she said. "It's an old one, and not very good. I think I can do this."

Not long after, there was a satisfying *click*.

"*Yes!*" Ariadne grinned and bounced up and down. Madame Zelda gently moved her aside and tried the handle again. This time the door opened smoothly.

All of us peered inside.

The first room was laid out like a kitchen—a very old one. There was a fireplace with a blackened stove and an ancient-looking pot. The flagstone floor was covered with leaves. There was a table, some broken chairs and little else. On the other side, the windows hadn't been fully covered up, and greenish light was pouring in.

Madame Zelda went in first, and we followed. The rain was tapping on the rooftop. I shivered, rubbing my wet arms. The room smelt of damp and forgetting and...wood smoke?

I peered into the fireplace. There were ashes in it, and when I put my hand close to them, they still felt warm.

At one side of the hexagonal room, there was a wooden spiral staircase. It looked as old as the rest of the building, though some of the treads had been repaired.

Madame Zelda leaned down by the old stove and picked up a rusty poker. She hefted it in her hands and then swung it experimentally, narrowly missing Scarlet.

"Hey!" Scarlet whispered.

"Should we shout for Miss Finch?" Ariadne whispered as quietly as a mouse.

Madame Zelda put a finger to her lips. "We don't know who's here," she replied.

As gently as we could, we followed Madame Zelda, tiptoeing up the staircase, wincing at every creak.

At the top, it opened into a very oddly shaped corridor. There was a wall, and there was a door.

Bolted shut.

Madame Zelda looked back at us, and we nodded.

She raised the poker, took a deep breath, and drew back the heavy iron bolt.

The door swung open, and we heard a gasp from inside.

And there, lit by candlelight in a blacked-out room, sat Miss Finch.

Chapter Thirty-Eight

SCARLET

I pushed past Madame Zelda and ran into the room. "Miss! Miss, are you all right?" I asked.

Miss Finch was sitting in a dusty armchair, a pile of old books at her feet. "Scarlet!" she cried, her eyes wide. "Scarlet, how did you find me?"

I wrapped my arms around her in a giant hug. I know, I know, it's odd to give a teacher a hug. But this was a special case. I was just so relieved that she was alive.

Ariadne and Ivy dashed in behind me. "We followed your map," Ariadne said, pulling out the scrap of paper from her rain-flecked satchel.

Miss Finch put her hands to her mouth. "Girls, I can't believe... Oh gosh. You can't stay here." Her eyes filled with shocked tears. "It isn't safe. She might come back."

"Who will...?" I asked.

But I knew the answer before it spilled from her lips.

"My mother," she said. "Miss Fox."

✻

The world spun under me, the floorboards threatening to crumble beneath my feet, but I held on. I wasn't going to let my fear get the better of me. "We didn't come alone," I said. "We have back-up."

I realized then that Madame Zelda hadn't set foot inside the room. I watched as she slowly stepped out from the shadows, and I soon realized why she'd hung back.

Miss Finch went totally white. "*You,*" she said.

Madame Zelda held out her hand, the other still holding the poker. "Rebecca, please, it's not what you..."

"*Get out,*" said Miss Finch.

"But...but she helped us rescue you, Miss," Ariadne started.

"I said I never wanted to see you again," Miss Finch said, shaking. "Get out."

Madame Zelda sighed. "Girls, I'll be downstairs," she said. She turned and walked away. Her solemn footsteps echoed down the staircase.

Miss Finch looked up at me. "Why is she here? Do you know what she—?" She stopped. "Never mind. That can wait."

"Miss, please, what's happened?" I asked. "Why are you locked in here? What's been going on?"

She said nothing for a moment. The upstairs room was as old and dark as the downstairs one, but there was a fire blazing in the hearth and several candles burning in holders. All the furniture was placed at odd angles in the weirdly shaped room. There was an ancient-looking bed with a quilt, a dresser, and in one corner, a battered desk with a typewriter on it. There were empty plates and cups on the desk as well as a pen and ink.

Something strange had definitely been going on here.

"We should leave," Miss Finch said, blinking at the door. She tried to pull herself to her feet, but quickly fell back down on to the chair with a thud.

"Careful, Miss," Ivy said, trying to steady her. "It's all right. Madame Zelda can help us."

Miss Finch frowned. "She's a fierce one, I'll give her that. But I don't trust her one bit."

"Come with us, Miss," Ariadne said. "We're taking you back to school."

"Thank you," said Miss Finch, the candlelight glinting in her tears. "I thought... I didn't know how anyone would find me."

Ariadne and Ivy stood on either side of her and helped her up. Clearly her leg still pained her, but she took a few steps with their support.

"I'll explain as we go," she said.

We helped her down the stairs. Madame Zelda stood at the bottom, poker in hand. "Rebecca, I—" she started.

"Save it," said Miss Finch, sounding more tired than angry. "Later."

Madame Zelda bowed her head. "I could help..." she offered.

"I don't need your help." I could see why she said that. Madame Zelda was the reason Miss Finch's leg hurt so much in the first place. But even though I found it very hard to trust her, I was starting to think she was telling the truth about being sorry.

Shuffling out of the front door, we found the rain had eased off a little. We took turns to help Miss Finch slowly back to school.

"What *happened*, Miss?" I said, as soon as we were out of sight of the creepy lodge.

Miss Finch's face was pale, and she was concentrating on the effort of walking. "It was my mother. I was in the studio, waiting for you to arrive." She glanced at me, and I felt a pang of guilt. "I thought Miss Fox was long gone, but she just appeared, right in front of me."

She stopped both walking and talking, and a look of horror crossed her face.

"She said that she was going to destroy the school, and that I needed to leave."

We all gasped.

"*Destroy the school?*" Ariadne repeated. "Is she going to blow it up?"

"No, I...I don't think so," said Miss Finch, and started moving again. "She has other ways of destroying things. But for some reason...she wanted to *protect* me. She wanted me to leave so that I wouldn't get caught up in it. But I said no."

"So, she locked you up in a tower?" Miss Fox was a real witch if ever there was one.

Miss Finch nodded. Her red hair was slick with rain and clinging limply to her face. Her feet shuffled in the leaves. Finally, we made it to the edge of the woods.

"I was too weak to fight back," said Miss Finch. "When I kept saying no, she knocked me out with my own stick." She touched a tender spot on her temple, where there was still the ghost of a bruise. "Brought me here, where I was trapped but provided for. She said she didn't want me to starve or freeze to death. I was frightened, and alone, but..."

"But it could have been worse," I finished. You always tell yourself it could be worse. Flashes of doctors and nurses and windows with bars on flicked through my mind.

She didn't say anything as we crossed the playing fields. Then she said, "She made me telephone to pretend I was all right. And she made me write that letter."

Ariadne nearly stumbled in the wet grass.

"She forced me to tell Mrs. Knight that everything was fine. I managed to slip in a couple of clues. I prayed someone would notice, but I was so scared that no one would, that no one would find me for years. I'd just be dust and bones..." She shuddered.

"I know that feeling, Miss," I said. She stared at me, her eyes searching mine. I looked away.

The further we got from the lodge, the more strength she seemed to gain.

"It'll be all right," Ariadne kept saying. "We'll get you to safety." I think she was reassuring herself more than Miss Finch.

"What about the rest of the letters?" I asked, when we were nearly past the hockey goalposts.

"She wrote them," Miss Finch explained. "I'd watch her sitting at that typewriter. Sometimes she'd read bits of them aloud. They were *horrible*. And she sounded so pleased with herself."

"Ugh, how awful," Ivy said.

"She didn't tell me much else. But a lot of nights, she would disappear. I think she must still have all the keys to the school. I could hear them jangle in her pockets when she moved." Miss Finch looked sick.

We carried on. "Not much farther," Ivy said, which was a bit of a lie. I could see Madame Zelda striding on ahead through the rain. She hadn't let go of the poker, and was swinging it by her side.

We neared the swimming pool, and saw its surface rippling in the rain. There were a couple of girls sheltering under the eaves of the changing rooms.

Miss Finch noticed them too. "No uniforms?" she muttered. She looked at the three of us. "What day is it?"

"It's Saturday, Miss," Ivy said. "The day of the recital."

"Oh my God." Miss Finch stopped suddenly.

"It's fine, Miss," I babbled. "Madame Zelda's got it all sorted, and everyone learned their parts, and, well, I've been banned from performing, but that's another story..." I was soaked and freezing, and I so badly wanted to get inside.

"It's not that, Scarlet," said Miss Finch, her eyes pleading. "It's my mother. She knows."

"Knows what?" We cried in unison.

"She knows about the recital. I think she's going to do something. And it's going to be something *terrible*."

Chapter Thirty-Nine

IVY

We finally made it inside the doors of the school, and all of us nearly collapsed with relief.

Madame Zelda told us to wait in the nearby empty classroom while she went to find Mrs. Knight. Miss Finch was relieved to have a chair again.

And we waited for what seemed like a very long time.

"What's taking so long?" Scarlet asked.

When she finally returned, Madame Zelda looked worried. "Mrs. Knight has already gone to Fairbank to meet with the theatre staff. She took the motor car. So, I called the police."

Miss Finch looked up sharply. "What?"

"They said they'd be here tomorrow," said Madame Zelda. She was standing in the doorway, uncharacteristically wringing her hands.

"Tomorrow? But that's...we don't have time..."

Madame Zelda protested. "I tried: I told them every-thing. They said it wasn't urgent. Apparently, there's been a robbery, and they don't have anyone to send."

"That's ridiculous!" Scarlet yelled.

"Are you *sure* you told them everything?" Miss Finch asked, glaring at Madame Zelda.

"Yes," she snapped back. "The stupid man said that being kidnapped by your own mother didn't sound like much of a problem. He said you'd been found safe and well and that was that. I told him that this Miss Fox was already wanted for past crimes and doubtless had committed more. I told him she might be going to sabotage the ballet recital. He wasn't the least bit interested." Her skin flushed red. "He kept saying he was a very busy man, he didn't have time for *fanciful stories* and that if we didn't know where Miss Fox was at this precise moment then it could wait until tomorrow."

Miss Finch was distraught. "We have to go to the theatre immediately. She's planning something, I know it."

"But how, Miss?" Ariadne asked. She had that look she often wore, halfway between fear and curiosity.

"I heard her muttering about the recital," Miss Finch explained, refusing to meet Madame Zelda's eyes. "And she made me tell her when it was. She's out to ruin the school's reputation any way she can..."

Madame Zelda looked up at the classroom clock. "Ivy," she turned to me, "please help the other girls with packing everything we need. We'll be on the bus at three, and we'll search the theatre when we get there. I'm going to make sure this ballet goes on without a hitch."

"Well let's hope nobody gets pushed off stage," said Miss Finch bitterly.

"Rebecca, I—" Madame Zelda tried again.

"Help me make sure the girls are safe," said Miss Finch, folding her arms, "and then perhaps I will listen to your apology."

Our strange new ballet teacher sagged against the doorframe. "Thank you," she said quietly.

℣

I had been afraid of going onstage before, but I felt even more afraid now. Imagining Miss Fox creeping through the school halls at night had been bad enough. Now there was a real possibility that she was staging some sort of attack, and we had no idea what to prepare for.

Madame Zelda had sworn that we'd be safe, but was that enough?

We snatched a quick lunch (that I could barely stomach, though Miss Finch ate with gusto), and the sets and costumes were hastily packed into hired buses. Scarlet and Ariadne weren't supposed to be coming early on the bus, since they weren't in the ballet, but with so many girls absent there were plenty of spare seats.

In my heart, I willed the bus to go faster. I wanted to get there, make sure everything was all right, and get the performance over with.

In my head, I wanted the bus to turn around and take us *anywhere* else.

The Fairbank Theatre Royal had a faded grandeur that was grand nonetheless.

The front was a series of arches, topped with the name of the theatre in gold. The posters that usually advertised plays and concerts simply read "Private Function."

I gulped and Scarlet took my hand as we stepped off the bus. I suppose all the drama had stopped her moping about losing her part.

We filed into the lobby and stood beside the ticket office. "Wait here, please, girls," Madame Zelda called. "I'm going to speak with Mrs. Knight."

Miss Finch limped inside, leaning heavily on her walking stick. "I'm coming too," she said, unspoken words hanging in the air. She didn't trust Madame Zelda either.

They hurried away to the auditorium.

While the others stood around chatting, Scarlet grabbed hold of Ariadne. "Come on," she whispered.

"What?" asked Ariadne, wide-eyed.

"Where are we going?" I whispered back.

"We're going to listen," replied Scarlet. "I need to know what Mrs. Knight has to say."

We sneaked away from the lobby and headed up the stairs in the direction of the main theatre. Scarlet pushed through the main doors, and we scurried in and hid behind the back row.

Inside, the theatre was even more impressive than the outside. Everything was golden, bathed in the glow of the stage lights. There were carvings of flowers and angels. There were hundreds of seats covered in red velvet that had been worn away by the sheer numbers of people who had sat on them. The stage was huge and imposing, a matching red-velvet curtain hanging down in front of it, golden tassels clinging to the bottom.

Our three teachers were halfway down the main aisle of the auditorium. Mrs. Knight had swept Miss Finch into a hug.

"Oh, Rebecca," she was saying. "How could this have happened? Can you ever forgive me? I should have believed those girls!"

I tried not to look at Scarlet, whose smugness was radiating off her.

"It's all right," said Miss Finch tiredly. She sat down on one of the seats and rested her stick beside it. "But right now, we really need to make sure the theatre is safe."

"I've called the police," Madame Zelda explained. "But they were no help."

Mrs. Knight gave a loud squawk of frustration. She was pushing her hands down toward the floor as if she could squash her mounting troubles. "It's fine. We'll be fine." She chanted it like a mantra.

"Can we cancel the show?" Miss Finch asked.

"Absolutely not." Mrs. Knight shook her head. "What kind of message will it send if we cancel? I had to slash the ticket prices just to half fill the auditorium. The show must go on, ladies. All the parents will be arriving soon. We're trying to show the best of Rookwood, aren't we?"

"But..." Miss Finch started.

"We'll search the theatre. We'll make sure she doesn't come in. It'll all be fine. Totally fine." I had the feeling Mrs. Knight was starting to go a bit batty.

"I think you're underestimating my—Miss Fox," said Miss Finch. She sounded both angry and frightened.

"Why would she come here?" Mrs. Knight said, oblivious to the tone. "She's wanted by the police. And this is a public event. But...*if* she does, we'll be ready. Don't you worry."

She patted Miss Finch patronizingly on the shoulder. "Come on, Zelda, let's do a sweep. When the other teachers get here, we'll get them to monitor who goes in and out."

She trotted away down the aisle, Madame Zelda following her. I guessed Miss Finch hadn't had time to mention exactly how she and the new ballet teacher knew each other.

Miss Finch suddenly turned around in her seat. "All right, girls, you can come out now."

Scarlet jumped up. "Miss! How did you know we were here?"

She gave a knowing smile. "I heard the door open. And Ariadne's rustling candy wrappers."

We turned to Ariadne, who had a gumdrop halfway to her mouth. "Sorry!" she said.

❧

An anxious few hours later, everything was set for the recital. The set was dressed, we'd rehearsed our parts, and parents were beginning to arrive.

Mrs. Knight kept insisting that everything was *perfectly fine*. She and Madame Zelda had checked the whole theatre, and there was no sign of Miss Fox. I felt relieved, but there was still the issue of having to get onstage and perform in front of everyone. Which was made considerably worse when I saw who'd just arrived among the parents.

All the dancers were getting changed on the upper floor, which had a balcony overlooking the lobby. My Diamond Fairy costume was beautiful—Aunt Sara had done an incredible job. It was made of light, silvery fabric with a flared skirt covered with pretend jewels. As I pulled it on, I began to feel just like a real ballerina. I tried not to notice the look of jealousy painted on Scarlet's face when she sneaked upstairs to join me.

I peered over at the people entering the theatre. And then immediately ducked down again. "Oh no," I said, hand over my mouth.

Scarlet perked up. "What is it? Is it *her*?"

"No," I said quickly. "Look!" I pointed upward, gesturing for her to look over the rail.

She did, and then she slid down beside me on to the plush carpet. "Ugh," she said. "Father and the step-troll. That's almost worse."

Our stepmother had always been nasty to us whenever she was out of Father's earshot, and we'd suspected she'd done worse. And Father...he'd never wanted us near him. We were a constant reminder of Ida, of his first love and what he'd lost.

"Why are they here?" Scarlet moaned. She knelt up and peered over again. "Oh!" she whispered. "Aunt Phoebe's with them!"

That was a little cheering at least. "Any sign of Aunt Sara?"

My twin shook her head. "Not yet. Anyway, I've got to go." Her face fell. "I've been put on *curtain duty*. With Penny."

As I took my place backstage and began warming up among the other girls, my heart was racing. I could hear the auditorium filling up with voices, and there was a blur of conversations from behind the curtain.

Scarlet slipped past me. "Break a—" she started. "On second thought, let's just say good luck, all right?"

I swallowed, and carried on stretching in a quiet corner behind the tall painted castle. The stage looked so different from here, all ropes and lights and scaffold with ladders leading up into the dark of the roof. When we'd practiced earlier, the lights had been on and the seats empty. Now we were in shadow, and the curtains were down, the audience hushed in anticipation.

It was really going to happen.

I took a deep breath.

And then a hand clamped over my mouth.

Chapter Forty

SCARLET

I took my position in the darkness. Unfortunately for me it was right next to Penny's.

Madame Zelda had quite literally showed us the ropes, with the help of the theatre manager. I knew what I had to do, but I wished I didn't.

It was *humiliating*. I was the best ballerina, yet here I was, stuck pulling up the bloody *curtains*. Ivy was wearing a beautiful costume, while I just stood here in my school uniform, hating every minute of it.

"This is entirely your fault," I hissed at Penny.

She twisted to face me. "Oh, is it now? You're the one who picked on me!"

"Because *you* bullied my sister and then accused me of poisoning everyone!" I whispered back.

"Shut up," she said. "It's about to start!"

I thought I heard a sort of thud behind me and a

noise over my head, but I ignored it. "Well I hope you're happy," I continued. "We'll probably never dance again."

"Oh, don't be melodramatic," said Penny. "Let's just do this stupid job like we're supposed to. Since it's *your fault* we have to do it."

I nearly slapped her, but suddenly Nadia appeared next to us in her Lilac Fairy costume. In the low light I could just see the little fabric lilac blossoms twirling around her tutu. She looked so wonderful I wanted to cry.

"Both of you shut up," she said quickly. "There's less than a minute to go. Where's Ivy?"

I looked around. "Over there, isn't she?"

From below the stage, I heard the music start to play. I took hold of the rope.

And that was when we heard the scream.

⅏

"*Ivy!*" I yelled.

It was my sister. I knew it. I dropped the rope.

The scream came from up above. How was that possible?

I ran across the back of the stage, my eyes darting around. I could hear Penny yelling at me over the music.

Ivy. Ivy. Ivy. I kept thinking her name like a prayer. What was happening? I had to find her!

Then I spotted a ladder.

Thank goodness I'm not in a tutu, I thought. I

grabbed a rung of the ladder and began to climb up into the darkness. It creaked and wobbled as I scrambled upward. The music swelled below me.

I finally reached the top, breathless, heart pounding, and peered over the edge.

I was at some sort of wooden platform, up in the workings of the theatre, surrounded by ropes and pulleys. A door in the wall led out on to it.

It was dimly lit, but I could see, unmistakably...

The tall figure of Miss Fox.

❦

I gasped, and then clamped my hand over my mouth. *She's here. She's really here. Oh no, oh no...*

I wanted to scream, but what good would it do? The whole theatre was being serenaded with Tchaikovsky, and they'd never hear me from up here.

Our terrible former headmistress was standing over Ivy, twitching the cane by her side. I shuddered and clung tightly to the ladder. Although she was in shadow, I could make out her ghastly silhouette—that hair pulled into a bun so tight that her face never moved, that shapeless dress with its millions of pockets. The shadow from my dreams flashed through my head.

Ivy was perilously close to the edge of the platform. I could see her hands gripping the wood, and the terror in her expression.

Move, I commanded myself. But I was frozen with fear.

"Why are you doing this?" I heard Ivy say.

Miss Fox laughed. I hadn't heard that sound in over a year and had never wanted to hear it again. I felt sick.

"All that busybody schoolgirl detective work, and you still don't know?" she said. Her voice was like fingernails on a blackboard. "You tell me."

"I-I don't know...I..." Ivy was stalling for time. I hoped she would catch my eye, but instead of looking in my direction, I saw her tilt her head up and look Miss Fox dead in the eye. "You cared about the school's reputation more than anything. You told everyone my sister was dead and you made me pretend to be her! And all because you wanted...money?"

Miss Fox tightened her grip on the cane.

"No," said Ivy. "That's not right, is it?" I silently cheered her on. "You wanted power."

"I'm listening," said Miss Fox. She was playing with Ivy like a cat with a mouse. She took a step closer.

"You wanted power, because they...they locked you away! And they took your baby from you! And when you had power over the school that was everything..." Ivy was shaking badly.

Miss Fox froze in place. The music carried on below. They were dancing underneath us, with no idea what was happening above their heads.

"You seized it all for yourself," Ivy continued, "and we took it away from you."

I started to slowly climb over the top of the ladder and onto the platform. Miss Fox had her back to me, and I kept praying and praying that she wouldn't turn around.

"That's why you're doing this!" said Ivy. "That's why you want to destroy the school's reputation. Because you can't have it anymore. You're like a... like a spoiled child!"

As she yelled that, Miss Fox roared and swung her cane.

"*No!*" I shouted and dived forward.

Ivy ducked and rolled away, the cane whooshing over her head.

Miss Fox spun around, and I went for her. I tried to wrestle the cane off her to dig my nails into her arms. "Don't you dare touch my twin!" I screamed.

Suddenly Miss Fox had grabbed my arms and twisted them behind my back. I wriggled and fought, the pain shooting through my bones. "Well, this is interesting," she hissed in my ear. "Both of you at once."

"Let go of me!" I shouted, at the same time as Ivy shouted, "Let go of her!"

But Miss Fox pushed me forward and held me over the edge...

And for a moment, everything went black.

I was on the rooftop at Rookwood. Freezing. Dark. The wind was howling. Miss Fox was holding Violet over

the edge, forcing her to look down at the drop. My heart pounded against my ribs.

No, came a voice from somewhere inside me. *That was then. This is now.*

I opened my eyes.

I wasn't Violet. And below me weren't the grounds of Rookwood School but the stage of the Fairbank Theatre Royal and the twirling heads of dancing ballerinas, with the audience in front of them. The scene swam before me like I was underwater.

"Shall I let go?" I heard Miss Fox say to Ivy. "I couldn't have hoped for better. Destroying Rookwood and destroying the two of you."

"You wouldn't." Ivy's voice was flat with fury. "You couldn't."

"You don't think this would be the perfect way to ruin Rookwood forever?"

Oh God, she meant it. I was going to die.

"I didn't go far enough, pushing Miss Wilcox from the window, poisoning your stew. But I had made sure that this public recital would go ahead. A terrible accident, in front of all the parents... It would be a tragedy, would it not? It would change everything. A most...*unfortunate incident.*"

And then Ivy screamed. Miss Fox swung me precariously and I flew across the platform.

But Miss Fox's strength was her undoing—I used the momentum of her violent force to fling myself on to the ladder. I slammed into the rungs with a thud, the whole platform shuddering beside me.

I looked up, panting, and saw Miss Fox raising her cane over Ivy, who was on the floor in front of her. There was an angry red bite mark on Miss Fox's arm.

Finally, she snapped. *"This is your payment! This is what you owe me! I lost everything!"*

And then, the door to the platform creaked open.

There, against all odds, as the ballet went on below, stood Madame Zelda and Miss Finch.

"You didn't lose everything," breathed Miss Finch. "The only thing you've ever had was right beside you all along."

Chapter Forty-One

IVY

Miss Fox's cane hung in the air like it was frozen in time. "You," she said. "Rebecca, you shouldn't be here. You should be..."

"Locked in a tower? I know, Mother. And you know who rescued me?" She pointed at Madame Zelda in between gasping breaths. "The person who broke my leg."

Madame Zelda frowned and then turned and ran. I prayed she was going to get help.

"You'll be silent," said Miss Fox, flicking her cane toward Miss Finch. "Not another word."

"I won't!" said Miss Finch. She swung up her walking stick and hit Miss Fox's cane with a loud clack, sending it spinning off to the edge of the platform. I could see her chest heaving as she breathed. "This is where you listen to me! *I am your daughter!*"

Miss Fox took a few steps back, her face contorted by her persistent scowl.

"Do you know what I went through?" Miss Finch demanded, blazing with feeling. "All you think about is yourself, isn't it? But I was abandoned. I lived in an orphanage. I've been beaten and bullied and worse. When I was adopted, I made something of myself. I danced and I traveled the world. And then my leg was broken, and it was all over, and I came to you for help. And *you should have cared.*" Tears streamed down her face in the dim light.

"I..." Miss Fox faltered.

"I'm all you've got in the world. And how did you deal with that? You mistreated me and lied and *attacked children* just to stop anyone finding out the dreadful secret of my existence." Miss Finch limped forward. "I just wanted a mother. What I got was a *monster.*"

I felt an ache in my heart. Scarlet and I had finally learned that our mother had loved us more than anything. Miss Finch...she'd learned the opposite. She'd found her mother, and she had become her worst nightmare. I crept my hand along the splintered wood of the platform and found Scarlet's.

I watched Miss Fox's face twist. The words had hit her. Somewhere, underneath that horrible exterior, deep, deep down, I knew there was a heart in there too. There was a mother who had been forced to give up her baby. She was an apple that had turned rotten from the outside in.

"I will destroy this school," she said quietly. I could only just hear her voice over the music.

Still shaking, Scarlet and I climbed to our feet, our hands clasped together.

"No," I said, trying to keep my voice firm. "You've already destroyed yourself. That is more than enough for one lifetime. Madame Zelda is going to come back up those stairs with help, any minute."

"So, you choose," said Scarlet. "You can go backward." She looked pointedly at the edge of the platform. "Or you can go forward. You can go to prison and pay for what you've done, and maybe... just maybe, you won't lose Miss Finch forever. Either way, this ends now."

Together we watched as Miss Fox sank down to the floor. She suddenly looked small, smaller than she'd ever been. She hung her head.

And as we watched Miss Fox's final defeat, far below us the dance went on.

❧

There was a solemn procession as the police led our former headmistress outside. All the fire had gone from her eyes. They bundled her into the back of the police van outside the theatre and slammed the door.

I thought my twin would be happy, triumphant even. But Scarlet quietly started to cry, and I held her close. Ariadne appeared and I pulled her into the hug too.

It was finally over.

Miraculously, the other dancers had managed to perform the entire ballet even with a conspicuously absent Diamond Fairy. But I didn't care a bit.

We'd defeated *her*. I felt a tiny flame of pride grow inside me.

Scarlet, Ariadne, and I had slipped into the back of the theatre to watch the final part of the ballet— the wedding scene. I wondered if Father and Edith had even realized we were missing from the stage.

As the prince and the princess married, the audience broke into applause. "At least I didn't have to marry Penny," Scarlet whispered to me, and I laughed as the final curtain fell.

Ariadne went to find her parents—the little owlish man with a woman we'd never seen before. Ariadne's mother was very tall and strangely glamorous with perfectly curled blond hair. She gave Ariadne a hug so tight it looked like she was being squeezed to death, but our friend seemed to be enjoying it regardless.

We walked past Penny, who was talking to a big man who I supposed was her father, and I noticed that for once she looked genuinely distraught. "I'm so sorry, Daddy," she said. "I let you down. If I'd got the lead role, Mama would've come to watch me, I know it. But now you're here all alone."

"Oh, you silly girl," said her father. "It doesn't work like that. I'm sorry."

"I know, I know," she sobbed. "I just want you to be together again."

He smiled at her sadly. "Here you go, sweetheart. I got you something." He pulled out a blue ribbon from his pocket, just like the one Penny had always worn before Scarlet tore it to pieces. He pinned it to her hair, and she smiled through her tears.

"Well, that explains a lot," I whispered to Scarlet.

"Hmmph," was all my twin said. I didn't think she would ever forgive Penny.

We couldn't put it off any longer. Our parents were waiting.

I dragged Scarlet down the theatre aisle until we spotted Father, Edith, and Aunt Phoebe.

When she clapped eyes on us, Aunt Phoebe tried to clamber over several other people's laps to get to us. "Oh, girls!" she cried. "I'm so pleased to see you!"

"We're pleased to see you too," said Scarlet, with a big grin.

"More than you know," I said.

Father looked over at where we were standing. "What's been going on, girls?"

Ah. Perhaps he had noticed that something had been amiss.

But at that moment, Mrs. Knight climbed up onstage in front of the red-velvet curtain.

"Thank you all for coming," she said, once everyone had quietened down. "Let's give the girls another round of applause for their wonderful performance."

The applause rippled outward.

"That is not all I have to say." The headmistress looked flustered, but seemed much more confident than she had been in weeks. "You have heard about the tough time we've been through at Rookwood recently. Mysterious accidents, threatening letters."

There was a murmur, and quite an angry one at that.

"Well." She took a deep breath, and straightened her glasses. "I'm here to tell you those tough times are over. The culprit was found to be none other than former headmistress Miss Fox. But at this very performance, she was apprehended by two of our most promising students."

I looked at Scarlet, feeling slightly horrified. But her face was lighting up. It seemed she was about to get her moment of fame after all.

"So, may we have another round of applause for Scarlet and Ivy Gray, who have been wonderfully brave in the face of danger."

We stood in the middle of the theatre, and all around us girls clapped and cheered. And then the parents began to join in. Their admiration flowed around us. My tiny flame of pride grew and grew, and I couldn't help but grin.

Together, we took a bow.

"Ariadne helped!" Scarlet yelled out, her hands cupped around her mouth. "And Miss Finch and Madame Zelda!"

There was more applause and Ariadne's little group

of dorm-mates jumped up and down. I laughed, delighted that my twin would share her big moment with others.

"I was somewhat short-sighted," confessed Mrs. Knight. "I thought these incidents were something I could handle alone. These girls warned me that something was wrong from the start, and I should have believed them. I should have confided in all of you"—she gestured around at the parents—"much sooner. I apologize to everyone who has been hurt."

There was no murmur or applause now, only silence.

"Rookwood School must be a safe place," she said, taking off her glasses and folding them. "And from now on, I promise you it will be. Miss Fox is going to prison, and she will never lay a hand on one of our girls again!"

And if she said any more, I didn't hear it, because the cheers drowned out the words.

As people began to filter out of the theatre, I saw Aunt Phoebe chatting animatedly to Miss Finch. I smiled, happy to see them both all right.

Father came over and took my arm. "Girls, I...I don't quite understand. Where were you?"

Scarlet sighed. "We'll explain later," she said.

Suddenly, our stepmother appeared by Father's side, glaring at us. "Well," she said, tapping her foot. "I'd like to hear why we came all this way for neither of you to be onstage!"

And I'd like to know why you let everyone think my

sister was dead, I thought. But that could wait for later too.

Before an argument broke out, I spotted someone important a few rows behind my parents and I dashed off to get her.

"Excuse me!" Edith snapped. "I was talking to you, missy!"

The person I was running toward stood up, her glamorous night-sky blue dress falling perfectly, and she gave me a big smile.

"Sara Louise," I said, shaking her hand gladly. "There's some people I'd like you to meet."

I led her out into the aisle, and saw Scarlet grinning slyly at me.

"And who is this?" sneered Edith.

"Father, stepmother," I said. "This is our Aunt Sara."

Chapter Forty-Two

SCARLET

In a heartbeat, our world changed. I had never seen our father look so shocked. I suppose that's what happens when you find out that your dearly departed wife had a sister you never knew existed.

"It's wonderful to meet you," said Aunt Sara, after Ivy had explained.

Ha, I thought. *She obviously doesn't know them.*

"And it has been such an honor to have the pleasure of meeting your girls," Sara continued. "I just wanted to say that they'd be welcome to come and stay with me at any time. It would be a privilege to have them."

"I don't know—" Father started, but Edith looked gleeful.

"Oh, they could stay with you *all the time,*" she interrupted, through a smile with gritted teeth. "I'm sure they'd like that, wouldn't you, *girls?*"

I ignored her, the poisonous toad, even though she was right. "We'd love to stay with you, Aunt Sara," I said.

"Excellent," replied our lovely new aunt. "Now, Mortimer," she addressed our father. "We may not have met, but I feel as though we have—I know so much about you. In fact, I rather hoped you'd be here because I have something to show you." She reached into her handbag and pulled out the sheaf of time-worn letters. "These are all from my dear sister. *Your wife.* You may be very surprised, but I think you should know the truth."

He reached out for the letters carefully, his eyes roving over our long-dead mother's handwriting...and something else changed. Color returned to his face, where I had not seen it for years. "...Ida?" he said. "But who is Ida?"

Aunt Sara took his arm in her own and patted it gently. "Come. We have a lot to talk about." And she led him away. The look on our stepmother's face was furious, and it was absolutely *priceless*.

I didn't know, but things would surely never be the same.

Aunt Sara had invited us to stay, and I couldn't be happier. When she met Aunt Phoebe in the theatre lobby they got on fabulously, and Sara had said that Phoebe would be welcome to come and visit any time she liked too. That left Ivy beaming.

306 ∞   SOPHIE CLEVERLY

Our new beginning hadn't worked out so well, but I had a good feeling about our happy ending.

We said good-bye to everyone and climbed on to the bus to Rookwood. Ivy and Ariadne both fell asleep on my shoulders. I stared out at the passing streetlights and the black sky speckled with stars.

Back in our dorm, I couldn't sleep. My brain was too awake. So, I did something I hadn't done since last term—I sneaked out of our room in the middle of the night.

I slipped through the halls and down the stairs. At first, I didn't know where I was going, but soon I realized where I was headed: the ballet studio.

The gas lamps were out, but I'd taken a handful of candles from the supply closet. I found the matches left on the side of the old candle holder and lit them.

Madame Zelda and Miss Finch had, well, nearly made up. They were never going to be friends, but I'd seen them talking to each other. I didn't know if Miss Finch would be full of horrible memories for her, just as it was for me. I wouldn't blame her if she wanted to take a job at another, much nicer school. With less attempted murder. But maybe...maybe she'd want to stay.

I stood in the light from the flickering candles and looked at myself in the mirror. The mirror me stared back.

So here I was. The girl who died. The girl who was insane. The girl who came back. The girl who saved the school.

The girl who ruined her chances, a voice in my head whispered.

I was such an idiot. I shouldn't have fought with Penny. I should've been on that stage.

So, I danced my part, there and then, alone. I could be Princess Aurora one last time.

This time, my *pirouettes* were perfect.

I didn't know how long I'd danced for, but as I collapsed on the cold floor, my nightgown spreading out around me, I started to cry. Who was I really? What did it all mean? And what the heck was going to happen next?

And then I heard a voice saying, "Cheer up!"

I lifted my head. It was Ivy. She was smiling at me gently.

"How did you—" I started.

"I knew you'd gone," she said. "Didn't you do it enough times last term?"

"Ha," I said as I wiped away a tear. "I wasn't crying."

"It's okay to cry," she said. "I'm not going to judge you, am I?"

I sniffed, sat up, and hugged my legs. The candles flickered around us.

"What's the matter?" she asked. She met my eyes in the wall of mirrors. "Why did you come down here?"

I tried to find the words. "Everything's changing. Everything that started with Miss Fox...it's over. And now we know the truth..."

Ivy nodded thoughtfully. "We're at a crossroads,

aren't we? This is where it all ends and more things begin." She paused. "Scarlet, I...I'm really sorry I kept everything from you. About Penny, I mean. I'll never keep things from you again."

I smiled. "And I'm sorry too. I'm sorry I didn't believe you about Miss Fox. I'm sorry for all the stupid things I did. I just..." I glanced down. "I don't know why I feel sad." I took a deep breath. These were feelings that I never usually let out. But I could trust my sister Ivy with anything. I knew that now. "I feel like I'm not in control anymore. And anything could happen."

"Anything *could* happen," agreed Ivy. "But that doesn't matter."

I frowned. "Why not?"

She held out a hand, and I took it and climbed to my feet. "Because we're together. Whatever it is, we will always be together."

I looked at her, face to face, and it was just like seeing that reflection in the mirror. She was right! Of course, she was right!

Slowly, I started to grin. The real Scarlet was back. I could do this; I could do *anything*, with my twin by my side. "Shall we dance?" I said.

So there, in the ballet studio, in the middle of the night, Ivy smiled back at me...

And we danced in the dark.

THE END

Acknowledgments

So many people have worked tirelessly backstage to bring this book into the spotlight. I'd love to express my gratitude to some of them here. My thanks go to:

Magical editor Lizzie Clifford for waving her wand over this book and helping to make it something special. Lovely Lauren Fortune, who helped greatly with the plot choreography. The fab team at HarperCollins, including Ruth, Nicola, Simon, Mary, and many more, who have supported the whole production.

My agent/fairy godmother Jenny Savill and everyone at Andrew Nurnberg Associates for helping to ensure that the show goes on.

Fantastic illustrators Kate Forrester and Manuel Šumberac—thank you for painting the scenery and bringing my world to life.

My fellow word-dancers at r/YAwriters, #UKMGchat, the Bath Spa crew, and the MA Writing Group of Wonders—always on hand to chat and give advice about all things bookish. To my followers and blog readers—it's great to know you're out there, and that I'm not playing to an empty theatre.

Outside of the publishing world, I'd also like to thank the supporting cast: my husband, friends, and family. Thank you for always being there.

And finally, to you, the audience—thank you so much for reading. Give yourself a round of applause!

About the Author

Sophie Cleverly was born in Bath in 1989. She wrote her first story at the age of four, though it used no punctuation and was essentially one long sentence. Thankfully, things have improved somewhat since then, and she has earned a BA in Creative Writing and MA in Writing for Young People from Bath Spa University.

Now working as a full-time writer, Sophie lives with her husband in Wiltshire, where she has a house full of books and a garden full of crows.